Karine Khodikyan

The
Door
was
Open

PUBLISHED WITH THE SUPPORT
OF THE MINISTRY OF CULTURE
OF THE REPUBLIC OF ARMENIA UNDER
THE "ARMENIAN LITERATURE IN TRANSLATION" PROGRAM

THE DOOR WAS OPEN

by Karine Khodikyan

This book was published with the support
of the Ministry of Culture of the Republic of Armenia under
the "Armenian Literature in Translation" Program

Translated from the Armenian by Nazareth Seferian

Proofread by Michael Wharton

Book cover and layout interior created by Max Mendor

Publishers Maxim Hodak & Max Mendor

Դուռը բաց էր (The Door was open)
by Karine Khodikyan

www.glagoslav.com

ISBN: 978-1-912894-48-2

A catalogue record for this book is available from the British Library.

Karine Khodikyan

The
Door
was
Open

Translated from the Armenian by Nazareth Seferian

GLAGOSLAV PUBLICATIONS

Contents

The Door Was Open...

Every time, one second before she took the key out of her bag, her fingers seemed to be covered in frost, and each time it seemed certain that the yellowish metal would touch her fingers and chafe some of the skin. But when she opened the door and the empty darkness of her corridor rapidly embraced her with greed, she would feel like she was growing acquainted with her own grave. And when she would stick her hand into the darkness with the same rapidity to find the switch and turn on the light, she would once again feel assured that being alone with death would not scare her.

She went quickly to the kitchen and dropped the bag full of groceries on the floor, took off her clothes and went to the bathroom. She undressed as she walked, such that her clothes lay scattered between the kitchen and the bathroom, while the fronts of her shoes faced each other near the bathroom door, looking like a pair of commas.

She was in the shower when she heard the phone ringing, long and demanding. That was strange. The people who called her would often hang up after three rings, because they knew that when she was home she would rush over, sometimes running, picking up the receiver before the third ring, because she couldn't stand hearing a phone ringing for long.

The pink foam slipped over her body and the near-cold water pinched her smooth and slightly sunburned skin. She clasped her hands on the back of her neck and gave herself to the water that hugged her body… Yellow spots began to shimmer at the corners of her closed eyelids, slowly growing into bonfires… Her body began to grow warmer, and the small, tremulous waves began to crawl upwards along her sleek legs…

The phone started to ring again, lasting longer than before this time. The everyday pleasure of her shower was gone – who could it be? The restored silence only sharpened her hearing, she was waiting. And when the ring burst out again (and it really felt like a burst), she pulled her fluffy bathrobe on her soapy body and jumped out. She picked up the phone and realized with unpleasant surprise that her hand was trembling.

"I saw you come home. Why weren't you picking up the phone?" It was her neighbor, a woman on the third floor.

"I was taking a shower," she tried to sound neutral, but she was wary – when was the last time this woman had called? "What's going on?"

"So you don't know," the voice at the other end of the line bubbled with satisfaction. "I knew it. Half the building could explode and you'd still be the last to know."

The drying soap tensed her body, and a lump formed in her throat from this unsolicited stress. She wrapped the bottom of her bathrobe around her legs, sat down on the couch and said, "So tell me."

"Of course, you have no idea that there is a serial killer in our neighborhood."

"Why would a serial killer come here?" Had she asked this most absurd of questions on purpose?

"You always ruin everything and never let me tell the story properly!" the voice exploded with dissatisfaction.

"Has he been around for a long time?" She tried to correct her mistake by sounding apologetic.

"This is the second week already, we're all panicking," the voice informed her, tasting her own fear yet again, "He's already managed to enter two apartments."

The silence stretching across both ends of the connection would suffocate her at any moment, such that she felt forced to loosen the collar of her bathrobe – there seemed to be no air left to breathe in the room.

"Do you know what kinds of apartments he chooses?" the voice said smoothly.

"Women living alone?" she said, unable to suppress a smile as she imagined the face at the other end, contorted with disappointment.

"So you knew?" the voice said with what was almost disgust.

"I had no idea, honest." She was surprised that her voice had been able to accurately translate her own sincerity.

"Well… you would've figured it out," her neighbor magnanimously accepted her sincerity, then added, "Keep your door locked."

"You think he'll come here?" She was angry, which surprised even her.

"We've seen some suspicious shadows around our building for the past few days," the voice had grown so serious that she thought it must be a joke, a bet of some kind made behind her back.

"Who's seen him?" She had grown indifferent.

"Does it matter? What matters is that he's been seen," the voice scolded. "In the middle of the night… towards dawn… someone has gotten up to drink water and has seen him… someone else has had insomnia and has stepped out into the balcony and seen him… Naked above the waist with eyes that glow in the dark, they say… like a cat's."

The voice faded away, faded and dissolved into the woman's accelerated breathing. And the room filled with the nightmare from the night before… She had been tossing around in the heat that previous night. It was very late when she had finally fallen asleep, but she awoke drenched in sweat just an hour later, her tongue feeling heavy and tasting of bile. Her eyes shut, groping the walls, she made it to the kitchen, opened the refrigerator door and sat down on the floor in front of it. Her hands made the familiar move to grab the bottle of water, and the cold water— with the pieces of ice floating in it—was unpleasant at first, she thought that lukewarm water would perhaps have been better. Her hand shot out again and grabbed a strawberry from a plate, which she brought up to her nose – the barely noticeable aroma had a trace of coolness in it. She crushed the strawberry and threw it back into the plate, slammed the door shut loudly and began to lick her reddened fingers. She got up from the floor, eyes still closed, and went to the bedroom, but swerved before she got to her bed towards the open door that led to the balcony. The wind didn't even offer a distant presence that night. She was about to draw the curtain back and step out into the balcony when something held her back. She didn't understand what it was, but the fear that was born inside her rendered her immobile with anticipation. The room, the heat and the night all filled with the same expectation. With eyes half-closed, so that her sleep would not slip away for good, she tried to look at the other side of the curtains, where there was darkness, but… was there only darkness? She shrugged her shoulders and reached out for the curtain. The immobile fear within her frowned in warning – where are you going? On the other side of the curtains, there was the heat of the night, but… was there only heat? She turned around and dropped into bed as the starched sheets crinkled in complaint. It was only when she lay in bed that she realized – her heart was beating so fast it was like it had come to a standstill. The yellow spots that sparked at the corners of her eyelids fused with each other and suddenly turned into the outline of a person standing there, on the other side of the curtain. She jumped, sat up in bed and looked at the near-black wall with eyes wide open. The same outline could be seen on the wall. At that moment, the room began to fill with the breathing of the person standing on the other side of the curtain, calm and even… Breathing so calm that it provoked terror, breathing so even that it caused goosebumps. A moment later, she was near the door, lurking in a shadow as she examined the darkness through a gap in the curtain. She went back and forth several times before she began to focus her attention on a tree on the opposite sidewalk. She couldn't see anything, but the breathing of the person there (she no longer doubted this) began to grow even more frequent. Her eyes began to burn, then teared up, and when the yellow spots hidden in the depths of her eyelids began to scald her pupils… someone seemed to float out of the darkness. She only managed to see his body, naked above the waist, and the light shining in his eyes. A second later, the darkness absorbed him once again, and his breathing was lost. It was in her dream that she saw his straight, powerful shoulders, his muscular neck… there was something monstrous about the body that had floated out of the darkness, causing terror and pleasure that enveloped one in equal portions of goosebumps. And the powerlessness born of these two suggested with disdain that one would probably not resist his bloody sigh in the dark…

She had woken up later than usual, and the previous night had seemed like a nightmare born from the heat.

"What happened? Say something. Hello, hello…" the neighbor's voice barely managed to break through the fever that had enveloped her, and it burst in her temples.

"What could have happened? I'm here, why are you panicking?" She said unapologetically.

"I've been sitting here for an hour trying to get you to make a sound, but there's been no reaction… I'm panicking, she says," the voice seemed to be genuinely upset.

"I'm sorry, I… the phone connection had been interrupted… perhaps."

"The phone?" the voice grew milder. "Yes, it's possible. What was I saying? Ah, yes. So the strange thing is that when he enters a house, the doors and locks remain intact."

"So what trace does he leave, is it…"

"Just blood," the voice warned, almost with hostility, "He does it with a blade… He rips the body apart after he has his fun with it. They say that, in both cases, he performs his task with perfection. Ah, my little one is here, I have to go to the kitchen. My point is this – being extra careful won't do you any harm."

"I'll use both locks on the door," she said as a final peace offering, and threw down the receiver, "Phew…"

The evening had been irreversibly ruined. She had a dinner of sorts and tried to get some work done, but failed. She switched the television off just as soon as she had switched it on. Then she went from room to room, aimlessly, without a thought in her head, the bottom of her bathrobe flowing, her soapy body tense and inaudibly rustling. Then she curled up in the couch and fell asleep, with someone's calm and even breathing in her ear. The darkness appeared in her dream, and then someone's body floated out of it, naked from the waist up. There was a monstrous power within that body, a beast that devoured itself with pleasure, ready at any moment to sink its claws into another body and feel the bloody pulsation of hot arteries in its nostrils. But that force also had powerful shoulders, a muscular neck, a sinewy body that could lose itself in a wave of mad passion, turning into a wave itself, driven insane by the aroma of love's moon juice. And the fear trembling within the woman calmed down and writhed with pleasure.

…the long ringing of the phone in the silence of the night felt like claws that were being dug into her temples.

"What's wrong with you? Why did it take you so long to get to the phone?" The neighbor's voice seemed to have a genuine note of concern in it.

"What time is it?" Had she asked this most unsuitable of questions on purpose?

"You've decided to drive me crazy," the voice resigned itself. "Have you closed your doors and windows?"

"Quite the contrary," she said and laughed – it was such a good laugh, girlish and sonorous.

"Good job," the voice grew jovial, "It's three in the morning." And it faded into the silence of the night.

The room swayed sleepily in the heat of the night. Without looking around her, she went into the bedroom and stretched out on the starched and rustling bedsheets, inaudibly swearing at her neighbor. Her swearing began to gradually adopt a certain rhythm and pace, which surprisingly calmed her down. As was her custom, she curled herself up into a ball and closed her eyes. The calm and even breathing came inside from the balcony and seized the room. She dug her head into her pillow, but not only did the breathing grow more audible, it began to lose its uniformity, its intermittent sighing moving the curtain, insignificantly at first, and then in waves. She got up from the bed and carefully went to the bathroom, throwing the bathrobe off along the way, while the slippers she left at the bathroom door, turned away from each other as if not on speaking terms, looked like a pair of semi-colons.

She stood below the shower and opened the hot water faucet to its fullest. The water hit her body and washed away the scales of dried soap, and the shackles of secret shivering that had imprisoned her body for years. And when her body was freed of the last of the shackles and it palpitated with a trace of dark blood, the water stopped flowing.

She left the bathroom and went to the bedroom. The breathing was no longer on the other side of the curtain. Clouds had appeared on one side of the sky and a slight breeze was picking up, there was nothing else. She breathed the smell of a waking day for a few minutes, then went back inside. The fear within her, eyes watching the door of the corridor, looked with anticipation – should I stay, or disappear? She smiled, put her finger to her lips, "Shhh" and reached out for the key, unafraid for the first time that the skin of her fingers would chafe when she touched the metal. And when she opened the door, the feeling of her own grave, which had grown so familiar to her, was gone.

I Wasn't Going

The ground was wet and muddy, sticky and without compassion. The fog born from the depths of the night grew denser and moister with each step I took. Around me, within a radius of around a hundred paces, there was an expectant silence, but I was certain that somewhere out there—far away or just one step away from me—the night owl lay in ambush, a harbinger of bad news… I had no recollection of how I had left home. I mean, what I had left had not been home for a long time already – it was a closed space that kept growing smaller and more cramped with each day, suddenly ending up like a noose tightening around my neck… I did not leave home; I snatched my body and flung it out the window, even though the door was wide open and I was alone at home, with nobody to stop me. After it was flung out the window, my body flattened on the dead grass, and my nostrils captured the mugginess of the fog that was growing heavier in the night. My knee smarted. I rubbed it and felt a sticky wetness, but the blood did not have time to cause pain. The expectant silence descended and covered me. The yellow light from the windows seeped out like pus and coagulated two inches away from me. The light did not reach me, I was in the dark, I was trying to persuade myself to get up and leave, but a debilitating stiffness had nailed my body to the floor. I had to leave, it was impossible to stay because the night was only just starting and I had moved too far from the dawn. A powerless tear rolled down from my tired eyes and I pressed my lips tightly – I was not going to scream. I don't remember how long it all lasted, but somewhere—far away or very close by—the owl awakened and the sleepy yellow light started showing signs of life, spreading out in a circle and approaching my feet. I looked at the windows, nothing had changed there, but the light flowing out now threatened to gobble up my feet. And I managed to escape.

The fog through thicker and thicker. How far had I come from home, where was I? I had no way of knowing. I simply walked, pursued by the sole thought of being able to escape.

My son, my child… You left home for just two hours. You combed your hair carefully, cast a judgmental eye at your reflection in the mirror and left, promising to return in a couple of hours.

I felt nothing. My heart had no sense of foreboding. One of those shows was on television; I was listening with pleasure to the stupid replies of the guests during the interview and chuckling… Oh God, I was laughing, while that villain, that bastard was plunging a knife into your heart. You gave a dull moan and then—your friends told me—you fell to the floor with that dull sound, while I was laughing… Why hadn't I felt anything? Why had you moaned so softly, almost inaudibly?

When they knocked on my door, I was not surprised at the fact that they had not rung the doorbell. They had knocked, echoing your dull moan. I straightened the end of my robe, opened the door, and saw your blood-drenched body.

You had promised that you would come back in a couple of hours, why did they bring you back after forty minutes?

After that, for so many days, I kept asking myself – why couldn't I shed any tears? Why couldn't I weep and scream out loud? Why was I only whining in a helpless and quiet voice? Why did I walk quietly behind the coffin, why wasn't I clawing my own face in anguish, why didn't I curse God? In fact, I did all that in my mind, with more cruelty and less mercy each time.

Several days later, the mother of that bastard showed up. The first thought that painfully skewered me was that we were both the same age, we were alike. We were both of medium height, with the same hairstyle, and we were even dressed alike – gray colors, no particular pattern. When I looked at her bent and hunched shoulders, I realized that I had the same droop. Her fingers twitched nervously as she folded a sweaty, crumpled handkerchief… My handkerchief was in the same state. She walked in sideways, silently opening and closing the door, and then leaned against the wall – her frightened, evasive eyes hidden beneath her eyelids, the elbow of her right arm held out as if to defend against an invisible blow. She was asking me to have mercy on her bastard. It was bad enough that we were so alike, now I had to show up in court and ask them to be lenient on that… on my son's killer…

I was by her side in a single leap. At first, I was just slapping her, then my hands reached her head and grabbed her hair. After that, my blows grew wilder, and she ended up on the floor, and I was kicking her whole curled-up body as she whined…

The neighbors rushed over and somehow managed to pull her out and take her to the other room, while I rolled around on the floor and howled like a she-wolf that had lost her mind at night. And after all that, she had the audacity to send the woman next door over to ask whether I had changed my mind.

I sneered at first, then I started to curse her. I covered my ears and swore hard, my unmerciful and fetid curses suffocating me.

And she, that bastard's mother, appeared in the doorway with her bloodied face and wild hair, saying,

"You are luckier than I am."

I was quiet. What could I say?

"I wish I were in your place."

An angry laugh exploded within me, but I managed to hold back, and even to speak,

"That… bastard of yours will spend a few years in jail and then he'll be free. He'll live through those years, and he'll be alive after them. But my son is gone… he'll never come back."

"Nevertheless, I wish…"

"Shut up. You're no less of a bastard! You've come here to mock my misfortune. Even if that bastard of yours rots in prison, he'll be alive!" I closed my eyes, helpless and spent. When I opened them, she had vanished.

I don't remember how much time had gone by, I had lost my sense of time. And now, I was walking through this fog and I knew that there was a steep descent nearby. Down below—far below—a river flowed, feigning sleep. I thought I would have made it to the descent a long time ago, but all I could see around me was the fog, which now seemed real enough to touch. I suddenly realized that I felt nothing beneath my feet, the ground was no longer present, but I did not have the sensation of floating either. I was walking on the fog. And so it went until the white fog gained a reddish tinge, until it turned the color of blood and exploded…

✳ ✳ ✳

[14]

When I woke up, the sun was at its zenith. The echo of church bells floated to me from afar. My temples throbbed dully, and there was the smell of blood somewhere within me. I managed to stand up with some difficulty, and looked around – I was out in the garden, under the old cherry tree. I stumbled to the door and pushed it open, entering. There was a half-drunk cup of coffee on the table and a plate with crumbs of cake. I was trying to remember what had happened the previous night when my son appeared at the doorstep.

"Mom, hurry up, I'm going to starve to death!"

Dreams aren't supposed to be like this. You can't experience smells like this when you dream; dreams are never this real.

"Mom? Is your heart acting up again?"

My son is so caring, so sensitive, every little ache I have drives him crazy, so I am forced to conceal the huge pain I feel.

"Mom? What happened?"

He's standing so close to me that I can feel the smell of his body, I can see the fuzz on his upper lip.

"What's that bruise on your forehead?"

I feel his fingers touching my forehead and I dig my teeth into my lips to keep myself from shouting.

"Mom? Hey, mom?"

He's so frightened that I somehow manage to say, "My foot stumbled on a tree branch… in the garden, a couple of minutes ago…" My words are far from convincing, but my son doesn't notice, he has already moistened a towel and placed it against my forehead. Then he forces me to lie down, changing the wet compress and holding my hand in his. I don't know what any of this means, but my son is here, he is alive… I kiss his hand, which smells of leather (he covers himself in leather from head to toe when he rides his motorbike), and I ask him,

"What day is it today?"

"Thursday, October 2…"

And I try to pretend as if I don't see how surprised he seems. I close my eyes and I try to keep my sanity. Exactly two months ago, on October 2, my son was murdered…

I managed to go to the kitchen and cook food. We sat at the opposite ends of the table, gulping down the soup enthusiastically and chuckling happily. We were both greatly amused by the bruise on my forehead. Surprisingly, it seemed to suit me well, it even gave me a certain mysterious charm.

I was doing some needlework later, he had closed the door to his room and was listening to music, and there was a second when I believed that the past had been a nightmare of some sort, that these moments were reality… After dinner, he hugged me and plunged his nose into my hair, and I knew what he was going to say next.

"Mom, I'm meeting up with some of the guys. I'll be back in a couple of hours, okay?"

Was I supposed to say no? I managed to smile and say, "Go." And he left, promising to be back in a couple of hours.

I tidied up the room, took out some rat poison I had kept in a corner of the kitchen and put it on the table. The clock on the wall ticked as the hands advanced. Twenty minutes had gone by, then twenty-five… I poured the poison into a glass and looked at the clock. Thirty minutes had passed and at that moment hurried steps approached the door. My son walked in, his eyes bright with an alien shimmer, panting, his arm bloody, a knife in his hand.

"I… a few minutes ago… I stabbed someone… I don't know how it happened. Mom, help me…"

The police will storm in a few moments later and handcuff him, then take him away. There will be an interrogation, then court proceedings… But before that, I would go to the mother of the victim and ask her to have mercy for my son… for my s… for that basta…

He was still leaning against the door, holding it tightly, as if he wanted to melt into the wood and disappear. His eyes—the eyes of a frightened and hunted creature—looked at me and I did not know what their depths held – remorse, fear, or… the warm smell of blood. I looked at my son, at my boy, who had never caused me any sorrow in my life, who had never harmed a soul, who was so concerned for my health that I had to conceal my great pain from him. My heart was breaking with compassion and hurt, but I did not want to visit the mother of the victim. I looked at my son… my son… that basta… I was afraid to go there. I could not go to visit myself.

I was very tired. The hands that fumbled for and found the poisoned glass were tired. The lips that drank the colorless liquid were tired. My throat was tired as it nervously gulped down the poison, but most of all, my heart was tired, extinguished even before it felt the poison. Perhaps my eyes were less tired, because they continued to see my son, leaning against the door. And I could not understand – was he the victim or the executioner? Perhaps my mind was not so tired either, because it knew that I would continue to be with my son. But my soul was at peace – I wasn't going…

Étude

"See," said the Man, "I can burn these papers. Until the very last, unfinished page. What would that change?"

"See," thought the Woman, "I could burn. Until the very end, until my last breath. What would remain of the fire?"

"There's nothing easier and more foolish than burning my papers," said the Woman, "And then, nonetheless, nothing would change."

"Well, of course," thought the Man, "What could paper reduced to ashes change if the secret of its destruction has been revealed?"

"I was kidding," said the Man, "You shouldn't take everything I say so seriously. Otherwise, there wouldn't be any books or libraries remaining in the world."

"No, of course not," thought the Woman, "It is only after the fire that something remains. Something important that nobody needs. Perhaps what they call the secret of life."

"My mistake is that I have never taken anything you say seriously," said the Woman, "I have simply believed."

"That's exactly it," thought the Man, "It's that belief that drains all hope away, at least when it comes to me. And what remains is the bad aftertaste of having said nothing."

"That 'simply' was well said," said the Man, "It gave a certain meaning to this tasteless argument."

"You keep mocking," thought the Woman, "That's what you're good at, isn't it? Mocking me, mocking yourself, and all that remains for the two of us in the end is the thorny space of unspoken words."

"Why did you separate the 'simply' and fail to focus on the 'belief'?" asked the Woman. "Perhaps because you have never believed me?"

"What is she saying?" thought the Man, "What is she talking about? What do I know about the meaning of that word? To believe… in your wife, your friend, God… Oh God, can't we do this without these meaningless words?"

"Perhaps I have not believed or perhaps I believed blindly to the end – what has changed?" asked the Man, "Or *who* has changed? Let's stop this, shall we? One shouldn't say so many stupid things out loud."

"What should I do?" thought the Woman, "How should I act so that I can breach through the fortress of words surrounding him? Damn it, it's true. I'm saying stupid things. I talk to myself the same way, like I'm on a stage, like I have an audience. But, wait. It's not my fault he's enclosed himself in stupid words and I'm forced to use equally foolish words to break through and find him on the other side of that fortress... somewhere."

"What do you propose instead?" asked the Woman, "Should we go visit someone, or perhaps go see a play? No, it's better if we walk arm-in-arm up and down the most central street downtown, attracting curious glances from acquaintances and strangers."

"Here we go again," thought the Man, "Why do women end up more merciless than executioners when their imminent defeat becomes obvious? Coming up next – she's going to wave these semi-secret rendezvous in my face like some kind of victory declaration. And, once again, I'm going to be the one to blame."

"Why are you proposing something you can't turn into reality?" asked the Man, "Aren't you afraid that I might take you up on that and drag you with me, arm-in-arm, up and down the most central street downtown?"

"I have to be careful not to be spiteful," thought the Woman, "I have to keep myself from being spiteful. Otherwise, we will once again be pushed apart by the thorny space of unspoken words (that has a ring to it – the thorny space of words... But if I use these words, he'll only start mocking me again by saying 'Here we go again!')... What was I saying? Yes, I should at least keep him from seeing that I'm being spiteful. When I become spiteful, my facial features grow sharper, I press my lips and make them narrow, and I grow ugly... I'm sure I grow ugly. And he doesn't like me that way – I know this for sure. In those moments he seems to... look at me from another angle. Like he's examining me... or trying to guess something, I don't know what. And my heart constricts in fear, like something unexpected is about to happen..."

"Why do you want me to hurt you?" asked the Woman, "To hurt you and end up hurting myself?"

"How she changes when she grows spiteful!" thought the Man, "She turns into someone else, a completely different woman. At times like this, I grow crazy with the desire to love her, crazy at the thought that there's another woman standing in front of me, a stranger I cannot understand. I go crazy to the point of paralysis in my mind and body. Only my eyes remain and they look at her unbelievingly, they love her and cannot get enough."

"You can't," said the Man, "You're too spiteful to end up hurt, you're too kind to hurt me. Isn't it better if we just change the subject? How come you aren't looking at your watch? Has your sense of time gone dull, or have you decided to extend your visit today?"

"Why do men go so weak when they think that victory is imminent for them?" thought the Woman, "And now he'll fling the blame on me of the bitterness that remains after these rendezvous. But why? Am I going to take the blame yet again?"

"If only you knew how tired I am," said the Woman, "Every minute I think about how I'm going to survive the next minute, and then a minute later I am filled with wonder at how I managed to survive."

"If only you knew how I love it when you start to think out loud with those half-closed eyes and fragile hunched shoulders, your soft lips barely opening and closing," thought the Man, "I've always had an explosive thing for philosophical women and here we are… I'm tangled in her love and those tormented words. Ah, now I'm coming up with pretty phrases too! Is she the reason, or are her words? Her words, probably, because I know for sure that I gave birth to them, through my weakness and difficulty."

"This is the perfect moment to demonstrate your profound thoughts," said the Man, "Don't you know it makes me want to explode? I said let's change the subject."

"How I wish he would understand me! How could I believe that he would ever understand me?" thought the Woman, "Perhaps that is why I'm here. And why I continue to come, each time without believing that I am the one coming to a secret date… He's turned around, looking out the window and seeing nothing. He's mercilessly swallowing the cigarette smoke and feeling nothing. How far away he is from me right now… But it is only at these moments that I realize how my lips go dry and crack with the desire to kiss him, how my fingers throb at the wish to hold him tight. This is truly a curse – to be madly in love when he's so far away… estranged. What would he do if I told him? Mock me? Hurt me? I don't know. I DON'T know. But I can console him with one thing – he can be sure of my love when I'm far away from him. How horrible I am… And how wonderful that he doesn't know how horrible I am. But what if he knows this well?"

"Let's change the subject," said the Woman, "What time is it?"

"Once again, I haven't been able to guess when she'll ask that question," thought the Man, "She always manages to pick the most unexpected moment. And, every time, something tells me to hold her and hide her till all the clocks in the world turn rusty… What if she found out the stupid things going through my mind right now? What would she do – smile? Take it seriously? I don't know. I don't know what she's thinking about."

"The time doesn't matter," said the Man, "What matters is that your time is up. Like every time… Look out and see the sunset we have this evening. What is that in your eyes?"

"Now," thought the Woman, "Now, I'll haul myself off this chair and go toward the door. Then I'll step out and keep walking… without looking back. Like every time. There is nothing in my eyes. Because I can't cry like a woman with eyes that have been penciled and painted. There's nothing in my eyes and, after I leave this place, I'll hide them behind a pair of black sunglasses. Perhaps you don't see that nothing, but the eyes of strangers can see everything. In other words, this is the plot from an old story—a fairy tale, perhaps—where the ending was obvious as soon as it started."

"Why do Armenian fairy tales end with three apples falling from heaven?" asked the Woman, "You don't know? All right, tell me a story you know."

"You'll leave," thought the Man, "You'll leave once again. And because I don't know when we'll meet again, I'll start to kill the days ahead—all the days without you—coldheartedly and carefully. And you'll never find out that you are the biggest murderer in the world. Because it isn't me you are killing, but the days I have without you."

"I don't know a story," said the Man, "What I know isn't a story. It's a funny and miserable tale. About how two strangers suddenly end up meeting and becoming the closest of couples. But they could have ended up not meeting, couldn't they?"

"Unexpectedness," thought the Woman, "This is the secret that binds me to him. I never know what he's going to say to me the next minute, what words he's going to use to hurt me only to deify me with the same words a few moments later. And these unexpected twists and turns turn into my source of patience – after all, I'm forced to live through the days when I am not with him."

"I also know a story," said the Woman, "But it is neither funny nor miserable. It isn't even cruel. It's about how the closest of couples suddenly grow apart and end up as even more estranged than before they had met. But they could have ended up not growing apart, couldn't they?"

"She's a woman who deserves me," thought the Man, "I can already see how this story will end. Well, at least there won't be any stupid explanations."

"See," said the Man, "I'll burn these papers now. All of them. Even the last, unfinished page."

"Try," said the Woman, "But start from the last one."

The Smell of Bread and Death

The first time he realized that his family was different had been before he had even turned five. He would live a few years more and turn twelve before he fully understood, before that wet, cloudy day when his father did not even look in his direction as he said in an unusual voice (or as he would consider later, a guilty voice), or perhaps one could say he asked,

"Come with me…"

But there was still time left before that day would arrive, and Avet, who was not yet five, would never forget the loneliness that invaded him when he realized that his family was living in that town with the stigma of being different. No, he didn't know that word yet, he didn't remember which grade he was when he read the word "stigma" in a textbook for the first time and realized that he had found it. His family's stigma… It was a week earlier, during the recess, that he had taken a piece of the pie that his mother had baked—which he had carefully placed on his books, wrapped in some paper, such that it wouldn't get crushed—and when he had held out an undamaged morsel of the baked goodie to the blue-eyed Mané, she had raised her eyebrows in surprise and had rejected it without saying a word. And as he had tried to understand why this had happened, Vardan, who sat next to Mané, had laughed,

"Would anyone eat something that you've touched?"

It was a week after that incident that he read the word "stigma" in a textbook and recalled himself at the age of five, and how he had cried. Even years later, when he would try to trace back when he had started to cry, he would be unsuccessful – was it the words, or the action that led to the tears, or was it a glance by a neighbor or a passer-by that had hinted to him that his family was different? But a cry welled up inside him and wanted to explode. There were no tears. It was instinct—what conscious understanding can one expect of a five-year-old?—that made him pick up the cast iron hammer that his mother had brought down from a high drawer to batter the meat, and bring it down hard on his left hand. His mother rushed up and threw the hammer aside with such force that it remained forever undiscovered among the distant bushes in the garden corner, and she put a cold compress on the hand that now resembled a sweet potato, forcing herself not to ask why her son had decided to harm himself. And Avet, who had finally cleared a path for his tears, watched all this like a bystander, tasting the burning saltwater, not knowing that this would be the last time he cried. From that day onwards, watching himself from aside would become a new habit he had acquired.

* * *

His father stood at the threshold, looked at the twelve-year-old Avet and recalled himself, but he had been younger—he had just turned eleven—when his father had stood at the threshold and looked at him… He ignored the hardened explosion within himself – there was no need to recall the past, this was the job that had been handed down to them from their grandfathers, and he was not going to flinch at the sight of his son's stare, nor would his hands tremble as he placed the shovel in the hands of what was still a child, and said,

"Dig…"

And his son would pick up the shovel and remove the first portion of soil from a plot that had been decided and delineated a day earlier, and he would be infected with the smell of a fresh grave and—like his father before him—he would never be free of it again.

* * *

Avet was walking over the footprints of his father. The rain had stopped a short while ago and the wet soil gladly took on the form of his father's misshapen shoes. Avet enjoyed walking over those misshapen traces. It was easier walking this way in the silence of the graveyard, watching it from aside, you would think that it wasn't him – just his father and his footprints. They approached the rectangle that had been fenced off with a rope. His father rested the two shovels and a pickax against the tree next to it, got down on his knees to feel the soil, and then stuck his hand in deeper. "What is he looking for?" the boy thought.

"Nothing to look for here…" he said, as if to himself, and the boy understood that he should avoid thinking in this silence, because his father could hear his thoughts.

"You will do the same," was not what his father, hand still dug deep into the soil, said. It was what he ordered.

"Do I have to?" he was surprised that he asked, and he felt convinced that he had known the answer to the question since the day he was born.

"The power of the soil to absorb death…" he grew silent and weighed his words in his mind one more time before saying, "That is the secret of our trade." Without waiting for his son's response, he rolled up his sleeves. "I'll start digging, then you," and he didn't clarify when that 'then' would be. The shovel went deep into the ground.

Avet watched his father – there wasn't a single unnecessary movement. "He's like a robot," he thought and then waited in fear. His father did not respond. So, when he's digging, he can't read minds. Or perhaps he doesn't want to…

It was a wet day, and there was coldness and sorrow inside him; the boy hunched up his shoulders – the shivering must not be noticed. He saw that his father's shirt was wet in his armpits and on his back. He understood that the 'then' he had mentioned was now, and he walked sideways to approach the second shovel leaning on the tree. The wood was so sleek that he felt nauseated by thinking about how many holes it must have dug. His vomit gathered in his throat, and he knew that he would either pick up that shovel and continue the job his family was doing, or he would walk slightly away and the bile and gall that would pour out of his insides would also free him of the stigma, and he would not approach the fenced rectangle that already emitted the rotting smell of decaying flowers. He didn't see it, but he knew that his father's hand was suspended in the air, waiting for his son's decision. Avet picked up the instrument and walked up while his father's shovel—as if it had never stopped in the air—came down and removed another portion of soil.

They emerged from the hole they had dug, sat down on the mossy gravestone next to it, and his father took out a bottle of vodka from his backpack and two pieces of black bread. Two glasses. He filled one finger of vodka in one, then poured the other up to the rim, and said,

"You'll drink today. After that, whenever you want to," he took a big gulp and looked away to avoid seeing the uncertain way in which his son was raising the glass to his mouth, and how he was trying to keep in the bile, gall and vodka all inside him after drinking what had lain in his glass. He waited until Avet, who was holding his breath, had swallowed, then smiled,

"You've become my assistant."

Avet would never forget his father's guilty, crooked smile.

* * *

When they returned home, his mother had already heated up some water in the large pot and had placed the wooden tub in the middle of the room in anticipation. They both took off Avet's clothes and together soaped him from head to toe, taking turns to pour the hot, very hot water on his head, until the bottom of the large pot became visible. They bathed him in silence, without looking at each other, and when their hands touched each other by mistake, they recoiled so quickly that the moist warmth in the room grew hotter. They wrapped the boy up in a large and fluffy towel and put him on the couch. Avet had not yet dried himself properly when the pot and tub had vanished, the wet patch on the floor was dried, and the samovar was bubbling on the table. They ate dinner in that same silence, and when Avet had mistily turned on his side in bed, his mother asked his father,

"What would you have done if he had thrown the shovel away?"

His frown came as a reply. His wife went to the kitchen so that she would avoid hearing the thought that had formed in her husband's mind, "There hasn't been a shovel thrower in this family yet!"

"But you've all tried to throw it away, every single one," she countered him, barely audibly. Later, seeing the fluttering eyelids of their sleeping son, they both knew the dream he was having – a shovel with wings was trying in vain to lift itself up, and those wings looked so funny and awkward…

* * *

In the morning, before he had reached school, everyone already knew that Avet had dug a grave. Nobody said anything, Mané did not look away, Vardan was quiet. But once he left the classroom, everyone would sigh in

[26]

relief. And it wasn't their fault that they were going to sigh in relief, the fresh graveyard smell that had seeped into him was not his alone… In the depths of the soil, Avet's hand had felt the power that his father had mentioned and knew that he would never be free of that smell. That very day, after finishing work, his father said,

"After you're done digging the hole, don't hang about. Go home."

"But why?"

"As long as you don't see who's being placed inside, what you've dug is just a hole, it's not a grave."

* * *

He was twenty years old when he did not go home after digging the hole. His father wanted to say something, but then picked up the shovel and pickax, and left without looking back. Avet thought, if I call out, he'll look back. This time, he'll look back for sure.

His father had once said, we don't look back in this place.

"Afraid of turning into a pillar of salt?" the boy had attempted to joke.

"Not a pillar of salt, but there have been those among us who had later seen the person who had just been buried."

Avet thought that he would never be able to make out when his father was joking, and when he was serious.

It was a hot spring day. He washed up with the water flowing from the memorial fountain nearby, and wet his grungy hair, sticking it flat to his head. He dusted off his clothes as much as possible and sat down near the hole. The silence, to which he had grown accustomed and had learned to ignore, suddenly made a sound… his heart was beating wildly. He saw that his hands had turned into fists, and he didn't try to calm his heart down, nor did he unclench his fists. The funeral procession was approaching. Marie had been dressed in red, and her coffin was covered in red roses. Marie didn't even look like she was sleeping, Marie was simply lying there with her eyes closed. Avet could not look away from the coffin floating above the procession and was trying to convince himself to believe in the fact that it had been an accident, and that Marie had not committed suicide. People don't commit suicide in small towns, and, even if they do… The coffin was lowered by the arms that had held it up, and swayed to and fro as it was brought to the rectangular hole that he had dug, before suddenly sinking into it… Avet felt the moment when the fear, which had not existed before, penetrated into him, blending with the smell of death. That day, he made his peace with the fact that he would be digging holes that caused fear and disgust until the end of his life. And there was only one hole he wanted to dig without fear or disgust. But he wouldn't dig that hole. No gravedigger has ever dug a hole for his own family.

* * *

Once he grew tired of sleeping with paid and unpaid women, once he was bored with their purchased or honest love games, he decided to get married. His father was long gone, his mother was not the same as before, the house needed a woman and a housewife. In this family, where only boys were born—and only one in each generation, all going on to become grave-diggers—there was also the habit of marrying late. His father had married in his forties, and he was approaching forty himself. The same way that his father had barely managed to persuade the girl and her family, he would also have to convince his future wife and her family. It isn't easy having a relationship with someone who deals in death. Just like his mother had never gotten used to the smell of death and had held her breath each time she got into bed and submitted herself to her husband's passions, until he would turn to his side and she would be able to take out a flask of rosewater from under the pillow, clearing the interrupted flow of air of the rotten smell of decaying flowers, so too would his wife hold her breath, except that her flask might contain something other than rosewater. The only thing that worried Avet was whether his future wife would be able to hold her breath for so long; his semen would arrive after half an hour at the earliest…

"Not just anyone can marry into our family," his father had interrupted one of the holes he was digging with these words, and he lit a cigarette, something he had never done before and never did again. "But we can marry into any family… if they want us," he inhaled the smoke and looked at the sky. "It's a good day, they'll bury her under the sun…"

They were going to bury a beautiful woman. Another accident. The butter that had been bubbling on the fire, supposedly turning to molten fat, had spilled all over her… Her husband, they said, had been in the next room…

Before that, they said, he had heard that in the months of his absence, someone else had come and gone to their house. But because he had been in the next room, the butter must have spilled by itself, burning through meat and bones. An accident. People don't commit murder in small towns, and, even if they do…

"The husband of the deceased loved her a lot, they say. He used to treat her very delicately. They say that, not only did he bathe before going to bed, he would even shave so that he wouldn't cause her any discomfort… But you know well the smell that the men in our family give off, no matter how much we wash up or bathe. No matter how long we are absent, nobody will come and go to our house while we are away."

"But why?" Avet was surprised that he asked, and he felt convinced that he had known the answer to the question since the day he was born.

"They say that the deceased is a beauty even in her coffin. The women that marry the men of our family can't be called beauties even outside of the coffin," he laughed through the rings of smoke that he blew.

Avet felt like he had taken offense on behalf of his mother that day. Later, he would confess that he had felt offended himself…

∗　∗　∗

It was his mother who first mentioned her name to him.

"Anette is a good girl for our family."

"Is she good, though?"

"Hush, now! There are no rumors about her in that way in town."

"Is that a good thing, or a bad thing?" Avet was asking this more as a way to tease his mother.

"For our town, that's the best thing," his mother had really felt insulted… was it only for Avet?

Avet was given a glimpse of Anette from afar. He looked at her, remembered his father, and smirked – she couldn't be called a beauty even outside of the coffin. He thought this, and forgot about her.

∗　∗　∗

"I haven't seen a man like you and… I won't ever see one," the blonde girl said, catching her breath. Avet looked at her, trying to recall her name. He failed. Blondie would do.

"You don't just make love, you squeeze everything out," Blondie began to think out loud, now more relaxed, "Every time you come here, it's like this is the end… like the world is coming to an end."

"What would you know about the end… the end of the world at that?" he thought and closed his eyes.

"If only it wasn't for that smell," she wrinkled her nose, "That smell lingers on me for a few hours after you're gone…"

"A few hours don't matter, just like you don't matter," but what he said aloud was "You, on the other hand, don't have a smell."

"What do you mean?" Blondie sat up, "The cosmetics that I use…"

"The smell of the cosmetics that you use doesn't belong to you. Your skin, your body, has no smell."

"Well, it's better not to have one, then…" but seeing the veins in Avet's sunburned and windswept neck stand out, her instinct of self-preservation forced her to swallow the words that were to follow. Then the instinct of a satisfied insect awoke in her as she said, "I wouldn't exchange you with a thousand others…" and she stretched herself out on top of him.

✳ ✳ ✳

Avet was walking down the street. It was a burning day in July. Everyone was hiding in any shady corner they could find. Avet enjoyed the silence of the street, which differed from the silence of the graveyard, but had a familiar feeling about it. In that heat and silence, he felt the smell of bread. The smell of freshly baked bread. He looked around. There was nobody. Then a woman appeared at the street corner. She was coming closer and each step of hers multiplied the intensity of that smell of bread. She was a stranger, but she looked familiar. Then he remembered – her name was Anette. When Anette walked past him, Avet lost his smell for a moment, the aroma of freshly baked bread was the only thing around…

That same day, Avet learned that Anette was a baker. A month hadn't gone by before he had brought her home. His mother's victorious glance, "I told you so…" was met with an uncertain reply,

"We'll see."

With Anette, serenity came to the home. She loved white, as if playing with flour the whole day wasn't enough, she replaced the flowery curtains in the house with white silk ones. One by one, unnoticed, the walls of the rooms turned white. The bedsheets, which were flowery in recent years due to his mother's age and fatigue, vanished. The white sheets, edged with laced and starched, did not provide a good night's sleep at first. Avet felt like their silence was like a continuation of the silence of the graveyard. But he said nothing. But Anette's aroma of bread managed to suppress Avet's smell of death, at least for a brief moment.

Avet knew that the boy who was going to be born would be his only child, but he didn't know that he would bring the smell of diapers into the rooms of the house. Coming home after digging a hole one day, he felt how the smell of death wavered, then dissipated when faced by the smell of his son's milk-and-piss diapers and his wife's aroma of bread. And then one day, he thought to himself that while there was no such thing as happiness, of course, there did exist something every similar to it.

When his mother died and was buried in the grave dug by her son, lying next to his father in a hole that he had dug as well, Avet felt that the smell of death had decreased in the house. With delayed surprise, he realized that his father's smell had passed on to his mother. He made love to Anette for a long time that night. Anette thought that he was loving her, but he was smelling every fold and pit in her body, inch by inch, trying to understand where his wife's smell ended and his began… Later, falling on his pillow in sweat and hearing Anette sigh as she took a deep breath, he felt that the aroma of bread that used to rise from her no longer had the same intensity.

* * *

The first time he took his son Vachik to dig a hole, he recalled his father standing at the threshold, and realized how difficult it must have been for his father to walk there, knowing that Avet was walking into his footsteps, as his son was going to do now. His heart constricted at the thought that the shovel would be stuck in the air in his hand until his son was forced to decide on the life he had to live. On the way back, Vachik kept tripping. He was drunk on a finger of vodka, and Avet knew that he would enter the house and see the large pot of hot water and the tub, and that Anette's smell of bread would vanish forever, accepting defeat against the smell of death emanating from two men.

That night, when he thought that both his son and Anette were asleep, he tried to dig his face deep into the pillow and cry like a baby who understood like an adult that nobody could comfort him, now or ever. He tried, although he knew that he had cried his last when he was five, and this made him feel very lonely, like his father and mother were lonely, although he had dug the hole for his mother in such a way that the coffins around her had ended up rubbing against their neighbors…

Anette, lying next to him, tried to breathe evenly so that she would not betray the fact that she was awake, and the voice of her mother-in-law echoed inside her,

"This family of men is very strong, that strength comes from the soil, which absorbs death. Every time they dig a hole, that strength seeps into their bones… and the smell of death emerges. I was like you too, I had a smell of my own, I even thought that I could suppress his smell. I was so naïve… When I die and I'm taken away from the house, only then will you know the smell that I gave to our home…"

Hearing Avet's dry, tearless sobs, she ended up discovering the answer to the question that had been gnawing at her since their engagement – why had that manly—handsome, even—stranger chosen her, a bland, uninteresting girl with clay-colored skin and lashless eyelids, whose breastless and hipless body caused the dress made by pauper Manik, the town's famous tailor, to turn into a piece of cloth with no form or color. And no matter how many times her mother said that the gravedigger was lucky that their family was free of superstitious and shallow thinking, Anette knew well how many widowed and married women had lost themselves in his embrace; the gossip going around without any particular destination had reached many ears, whispering the unusual power that Avet displayed in the bedroom…

Hearing her husband's dry, tearless sobs and recalling the words of her deceased mother-in-law, Anette had goosebumps – would she be able to suppress the smell of death that had taken up abode in that house?

* * *

When the neighbors found out that Anette was sending her son off to study, they didn't believe it at first (what else could this family do except dig holes?). Then they asked each other in confusion, who would dig their holes, then? One day, one of them gathered the courage to ask Anette that question.

"There's always been someone to bury the dead in the past, there will always be someone in the future as well," Anette smiled.

The person asking that question had a coughing fit, a reaction to the cloud of flour that had appeared in the air from seemingly nowhere…

The years went by. The holes that Avet dug were perfect rectangles as always, with a smooth floor, but he had grown old and crooked, walking with difficulty. But the years seemed to pass Anette by, especially since the day when she took her two-year old son Vachik to daycare and returned to her work, ignoring the complaining whispers of the people around her about how Vachik was the only child in daycare from the town and the rest were all the children of the frivolous wives of the army officers at the local base. Nobody worked as hard as Anette. She was the first to arrive at the bakery and the last to leave. She would knead the flour with such care that one would think she was preparing for the New Year meal. She would return home with the flour not yet dusted off her, and with traces of dried dough even on her wrists. She walked home lightly at dawn, as if it hadn't been her kneading large vats of dough all night, making hundreds of little balls. And she ignored the comments that floated about her – 'Isn't Avet seeing any of this?'

Avet was growing weak and fading. Anette was blooming, her skin had lost its former clay color and had taken on a milky sheen. She had straightened and spruced up, such that the dress that the now-deceased pauper Manik had sewn years ago now hugged her desirable body. The neighboring women tried to find a cause behind all this but would retreat in the face of Avet's silence and Anette's smile, searching for an answer among themselves. Only one of them would find the strength within herself to ask Anette this question, but recalling the constriction and suffocating cough that had resulted from the cloud of flour that had suddenly appeared the last time, she kept herself from suspecting anything, much less speaking about it.

Avet took on an apprentice. They found an orphan boy and said, the town is counting on you once Avet dies, learn from him. Would Avet teach him to dig a hole? The boy began to learn… and dig. And Avet, an unlit cigarette in the corner of his mouth, would repeat the things that he had heard from his father about not looking back, not being part of the funeral after digging the hole… and many other things. One day, he made up his mind and came home after digging a hole, stood on the threshold and said,

"Call Vachik…" but he didn't continue.

"Why?" Anette understood.

"If I'm not going to dig my own hole, at least my son should do it. That will be some consolation, at least," he laughed through the rings of smoke, walked up and kissed his wife. Anette didn't have enough time to hold her breath and felt her husband's warmth for the first time in thirty years. And only once Avet had left did she realize that she had felt no nausea.

*　*　*

The neighbors couldn't understand why Anette kept working. Avet received a pension and their son sent a lot of money back home. Why did she go to bake bread every night? She didn't even do any of the baking herself, her hands were no longer strong enough. All she did was go there, give advice, and hold the dough.

Avet was bedridden after the stroke. But Anette kept going to bake bread every night, until one day at dawn when she entered the house and saw Avet's look of gratitude. She understood what he wanted to say to her. The only smell in the house was that of bread, the bread baked that night, with dough that Anette had kneaded with tears as she gathered every ounce of strength in her hands. The woman sat down next to her husband, took his hand and helped him through his final seconds, whispering the words that would show the way to the start of the final journey, and she managed to hear his final thoughts in his fading eyes. Anette knew that her Avet was at peace because only the smell of bread remained in the house, while the smell of death that had become a stigma for the family, had just left the house a moment ago and was searching for a new abode.

Anette closed Avet's eyes and kissed his lips, without holding her breath for only the second time in thirty years. Then she got up and made a phone call to her son.

Five Cars off the Side of the Road

The valley stretched out on the right side, the left side was carved out of the foothills and the highway only opened out after the bends in the road were done, but less than one hundred meters after that the scenery shut off again and turned into a stretch of paved road and a cliff dropping off into the valley.

The man lay on the elevated curb, his face looking up at the sky, his arms held out wide. His position was suggestive of a carefree person who was relaxing on a summer day, but his bare soles seemed to hint at something else to the people glancing out of the cars that sped past him. The man could just be seen in that hundred-meter space, and only by the cars going downhill on the road. But anyone looking out the window had a few minutes to register how the man had stretched out his arms broadly, held out his legs straight, and had unnaturally white soles, the whiteness of which seemed to hide something shameful. To someone with a wild imagination, the man lying on the elevated curb could be reminiscent of a cross lying in the sunburnt soil…

* * *

"My robe… I knew I'd forgotten something… But where was it, how could I have missed seeing it?" The woman lowered the window and threw out her cigarette.

"What's the ashtray for?" the man turned his eyes away from the road for a moment, pressed a button, and the window silently slid back up, "You know how angry I get when people throw all kinds of things out of car windows and…"

"But what if I like it?" the woman seemed to smile.

"Even more reason not to throw anything out," he said, waiting for her response.

The woman lowered the window again and pushed her face out into the wind.

"*What does he mean by that? Did I upset him? No, this is just a grudge from last night,*" the man's hand stretched out automatically towards the pack of cigarettes, his hands expertly picked out a cigarette and brought it to his lips. Just as his hands were moving out again to pick up a lighter, he remembered that he had quit smoking. His foot slammed on the gas and the car picked up speed.

"*It's strange that I forgot my robe. It was the only thing I had bought specifically for this trip,*" the woman picked the cigarette out of the man lips and threw it out, "Patience. At least wait for forty days to go by from the day you quit smoking."

"It's been forty days already, and five days extra."

"That won't do. If you've been counting the days, it means you'll start the habit again."

"This time it's final. You don't believe me?"

"I believe you," she raised the window and silence descended upon them. "I believe you," she said more softly, then turned and put her head in the man's lap and, like every time, the sunburnt July sky poured in from the windshield.

The man's right hand slid down in a familiar motion to the woman's face. The woman kissed his hot palm and closed her eyes. And suddenly, it became very important for her to remember the corner of their rented villa in which she had left her robe. "The bathroom? No, it was white from floor to ceiling, I would have spotted my blue coat there. On the couch, perhaps? Or in the bedroom?" She was trying to picture the rooms in her mind, the items in them, everything that belonged to the two of them for the four days they were there. After three years of being with each other, they had finally shared a room and a bed together…

"Where did those three years go?" she said and was amazed at how her thought had been voiced out loud.

"Indeed," the man's voice held no surprise.

"*Three years of secret and semi-secret dating. And only during the day, until seven in the evening at best, because coming home later than that would require some sort of explanation. There had been no reason for any explanations over those three years, I was never late… Is that a good thing,* or a bad one? What is he thinking? I'm not going to say anything. Let him think that I've fallen asleep."

"Is she asleep? How am I supposed to tell? She's an expert at playing dead," the man's hand slipped lower and rested on her breast. His desire to smoke grew irrepressible. The face of the woman on his knees, rocking slightly in harmony with the car's motion, was the one he loved and knew well, but there was a panic in his heart… "Together day and night for the first time in three years… and that ridiculous situation…"

"What are you thinking?" his voice sounded unexpectedly loud even to himself.

"I forgot my robe."

"The blue one?"

"Yes, I was trying to figure out where I'd left it."

"On the balcony," the man's voice went dull, "Last night…"

"The balcony. Yes! That's where I left it, on the floor… Interesting that he remembered it. Not bad, then he probably remembers the rest as well." She sat up suddenly.

"You should have slept a bit more, we'd be back in town before you woke up," he said, almost indifferently.

"I wasn't sleepy anymore," the woman said.

"She didn't sleep last night either. We were like little children, lying next to each other, pretending to be asleep," the man recalled and felt hurt. Then he felt that perhaps it wasn't he who was hurt, but rather his male ego. How could this woman, who was fully his, lie next to him all night and… pretend to be asleep? The woman opened her bag. The more carefully she freshened her makeup, the more the man grew upset.

"The worst thing at a wedding is the sound of the zurna. It's so shrill, it's like a harbinger of the surprises ahead for the newlyweds," the woman said. Even the sound of the river could not drown out the music coming from the other bank.

"Why do you say that?" the man stretched out on the rocking chair objected lazily. "It's not such a bad thing compared to the best man, the toastmaster and the rest of them."

"Did you have a *zurna* playing at your wedding?" she asked and thought that this was the first time since they were together that she was attempting to find out something about his life.

"Of course. And a best man, and a toastmaster…"

"And a bride who would lose her virginity?" she had not wanted to ask this question, it had popped out by itself.

"Do you have any doubts on that front?" he added a self-satisfied emphasis despite himself.

"Was the bride pretty?" the woman asked, all jokes aside.

"Very much so," the man responded.

The sounds of the people celebrating at the restaurant grew clearer.

"Pretty?" the man asked himself a little later, "I don't know… she seemed scared… That's the image in my memory – a scared girl in a white dress," he said and stared. What was that he saw in the eyes of the woman looking at him?

"Could you slow down a little?" the woman pulled the pencil back from her face with a nervous movement.

"Why?"

"I'm applying makeup around my eyes."

"As if your eyes needed any makeup…" he slowed down. "Should we go back?"

"Where?"

"Your robe…"

"No," it sounded rude, "I hadn't liked that robe from the very beginning. What is… look here…" the woman was happy that she did not need to continue the conversation.

"Where?" he also spotted the man lying on the curb. "It's a guy."

"Of course it's a guy, it's not an animal." The bare soles of the man on the ground seemed to be mocking the people who saw them. "But… something's not right. Why is he lying under the sun?"

"He's lying there because…" The man stopped the car suddenly and opened his door, "We're about to find out."

"What are you doing?" she grabbed at his arm, "What are you doing?" she asked more calmly.

"I want to see whether…"

"What do you want to see?"

"Perhaps he needs help…"

"Well, look at this savior! Leaping out with no concern for himself…"

"What's gotten into you?" he said in surprise as he looked at her angrily twitching face.

"So you can get out there and help the first person you come across? Have you ever tried to help me? Have you ever even thought of asking me how I've managed to survive these lies, the fear that someone would see us together someday? What's the matter? Are you trying to convince me that you can show compassion for a complete stranger when you don't even care how I feel? Where are you going? Get back in your place!"

"What's wrong with you? Why the histrionics?"

"You've hurt me," she coiled up inside and could not keep a steady voice, "Take me home!"

"What do you mean?"

"Take me home!"

"You say that as if you have somewhere else you could go."

"That doesn't mean you can make fun of me."

The man started the engine and glanced out of the corner of his eyes. The woman had buried her face in her arms and seemed to have frozen. *"She'll just keeping sitting like that. She won't say a word, she won't look up… I thought she was stubborn, but I realized a long time ago that this is just self-defense. Powerless self-defense. She's frozen like that and she'd rather die than shed a tear. Oh, how she wanted to cry last night! She wanted to slam her head from wall to wall, but what did she do? She stood in the middle of the balcony and slipped her robe off. Her body emanated light, perhaps it was the full moon, or something else… I wanted her to come close to me, oh, how I wanted her to come closer, but she…"*

"What were the words you had used? 'This is the first and last time you're seeing me and the moon at the same time.' Not bad – which book had you read that in?" The weakness in the man's voice made his words even more hurtful.

"Take me home," the woman said through her solitude.

＊　＊　＊

The house was writing in the heat. The woman took a deep breath – there was nobody home. She left her suitcase in the corridor, turned on the air conditioner, and went into the bathroom. She let the water run and the mirror fogged over in a few minutes. She wiped it with her palm; the woman staring back at her from the mirror was a stranger, uncommunicative. She carefully hung up her dress and gingerly stepped into the water – she couldn't stand it when her hair was wet. She closed her eyes, the only thing she wanted was not to think. And not to cry. Only splashes of water could be heard in the silence. She felt an unpleasant moisture, her hair was wet. She twitched nervously to grab the hair dryer from the drawer, and she plugged it in. It was a pleasant feeling – the warm water around her body, the cold air blowing in her face. She closed her eyes and tried to recall the man that had belonged only to her in the past three days. She failed. She shut her eyes tightly and opened them – a pair of feet appeared before her eyes… bare soles… she did even manage to register any surprise at why she had remembered the man on the curb at that particular moment… or, rather, his bare feet… She grew tense, tried to concentrate, and failed to notice how she slid underwater, the plugged blow dryer still in her hand…

* * *

"That's all right, you'll be luckier next time," he spat out the words and held out a hand. He also smiled, his yellowed teeth the color of rust. He seems certain that I'll shake his stinky hand, and that I'll smile, I'll definitely smile, although he knows well that the only thing I want right now is to strangle him, but not with my hands. My hands are too good for a job like that, they deserve better. I'll dig my teeth—my healthy, white, sharp teeth—into his throat and… My eyes grow red as I feel the rotten taste of his blood… I shake his hand, I smile.

"I'm always lucky," I'm happy, my voice doesn't betray me. "I can still call the bank," I look at my watch, I do this on purpose. Let that piece of shit notice that my watch is not a cheap one, and that the buttons on my shirt contain gems and are handmade items. I manage to catch him glancing – he's seen them. I feel relieved, although my behavior is puerile; he knows better than I do that business has not been *bad* for me. Business has been *very bad* for me. I'm on the verge of bankruptcy.

"Yes, I can still call them," is it just me, or is there a double meaning to what I'm saying?

But there's no need to focus on that, what matters now is saving face in the literal and figurative senses of that phrase.

"Until next time," I extract my hand from his sweaty paw and demonstratively wipe it with a handkerchief. His face grows tense, perhaps he disgusts himself too. I turn to the door.

"Wait."

I look back over my shoulder. Look at him, he can resist my stare!

"You remember back in our second year at college…" he doesn't continue, he waits for me to remember.

Will you look at that? We took the same classes for five years and I had not even spoken to him a total of five times back then. Now he expects me to remember the things *he* said?

"During Ayvazyan's lecture…" and he waits again.

Keep waiting, you're going to have to wait a lot longer than that, because you did not exist for me back then. Why would anyone notice a worm?

"You said…" Was it just me or was he smiling?

I wonder what I'd said…

"There are two kinds of people – human beings and the colorless." The silence grows longer and he is forced to continue. "And you looked at me."

"At which word."

"Colorless."

Oh wow, so he's also a masochist?

"Is that why you made sure this deal fell through?" Now it's his turn to be quiet. My voice sounds great – it's got a steely ring to it. "Yes, I'm in serious trouble, but you're also losing money. A lot of money." He is no longer smiling. "I'm not going to lose, but you're going to regret this," I say this and I realize how funny I am, and not just to him. He knows about the state of my business better than I do… or rather, I've fallen into a trap that he has set. Having lost my self-control, I flee the scene. My car is not there. I see red, the smell of blood awakens in my nostrils… I manage to fight down the tremor in my hands and I open my eyes – my car is on the other side of the street, where I had left it. Before getting in, I turn around. He was looking down from the second-floor window, but I could not see his face. The steering wheel brings back my composure – thanks to the breath of my pricey car penetrating to me through its expensive leather. The sensitive wheel just needs my slightest touch to tell the engine that I want to speed away. I have breathed something into all of my cars, I have treated them like pedigree Arab stallions… I drive out of the city.

"You have a good memory, you son of a bitch, will you look at how he remembers all that? I couldn't recall any of it if my life depended on it, but it sounds like something I would have said. Back then I would slash left and right with that sword of a tongue – who dared speak against and face my father's wrath? You filthy motherf… so you've kept a grudge, have you? You're the embodiment of drabness and you will always be colorless. You've got millions now, but aren't you wearing the same clothes? That same wrinkled coat? That's you! Ooh, but it must have burned him so badly then if he remembers it after all this time… And he'll remember it to the day he dies because I am me, and he's just some whore's pup. Because my parents have been good people while he doesn't even know his father's name. And the more millions he piles on, the more they will recall his mother's real name… And his mother… I have to get to the bank. It's all right, there are so many ideas in my head. All I need to do is survive for a couple of months and everything will fall into place. I'll bring back everything I lost and then some… There's no other way, there will never be another way, because I must lead the good life, people like me rule the world, my family cannot get by with nothing. How fast am I driving? 220 kph… Ok, calm down… 150 is fine, your car can take it without a sweat. Take a deep breath, there's nothing serious, everything's going to be all right. I just need to get there on time… Who's that? Look at him just lying there, the son of a… Sticking his feet out and just lying there under the sun, without a care in the world… Son of a… look at his bare feet just sticking out there! He's asleep, but it looks like he's dead. Either way, he's lucky. If he's dead, his struggle in this life is over. If he's asleep, may God have mercy on the souls of his forefathers if he can sleep this soundly. Not me – I need to bring back the money I lost, send my son abroad to study, find my daughter someone to marry, pay to have plastic surgery done on my good-for-nothing wife… I need money too, lots of money! You only live once… But that guy really went blue in the face when he saw my watch! His is definitely from back in his times at the Communist Youth Organization, I would bet him on that and win!

Here's the bank… I need to get that loan, call Moscow and tell them to ship the goods… Yes, it will all work out. That son of a bitch will grovel at my feet yet. I have no words for him, but he's the one who will come to me this time, to hear what I have to say."

"No, that's not possible…" The asshole at the bank is trying to speak calmly, but his eyes are rolling around in his sockets! "We cannot consider providing you with a loan."

"Listen here… I mean, please hear me out…"

"Let's not waste any time, sir." Ah, his voice is firmer now, it isn't trembling anymore.

"Is it him? You can't give me a loan because he said not to?" I force him to look into my eyes.

"Yes," I think I sense pity in his eyes. You son of a… "There's nothing you can do. He's blocked every option you have." Perhaps he has held out a hand, he might even be smiling, but all I can see is red, and feel the salty taste of blood in my nostrils.

There's nobody in the office. Good. I close the door. I lock it. I've always thought about what the last thing would be to cross my mind. Or perhaps, the last person. The barrel of the gun stares at my face unblinkingly. I'll wait until the last thought or memory appears beneath my eyelids. It is red, smelling of blood and red, and then the red grows slowly paler and becomes yellow, it becomes a sunburnt day in July, and then lines and dots appear, randomly slamming into each other, as if trying to turn into something. My hand has grown heavier, the barrel of the gun is hotter. I'm waiting. Ah… someone… has appeared. Who is it? Is it a stranger? Who do you see at that very last moment? What is that person doing? Lying on the ground… where? On the curb? And his feet… bare. But why am I seeing him in my final moment? Is this the end?

* * *

"I've told you a thousand times – don't read in the car. You'll ruin your eyesight," the mother said softly, without any emotion, saying it as if she were patting her head lightly, but then giving a slight tug to a bunch of hair on her daughter's head. "I thought you'd heard me the first time."

"She heard you," the father of the fifteen-year-old girl sitting in the back smiled as he glanced at her through the rear-view mirror. "She heard you. But if she can't read, what is she supposed to do?"

"Look around. We're losing it in the city – we can't see beyond our own noses. Flowers, trees, natural landscapes – we don't see any of this. But we've become really good at noticing the houses and guesthouses that others build."

"Hotels," the girl corrected her, knowing that this would irritate her mother. Then she put the magazine on her knees and demonstratively stuck her nose to the window. "What is there to see here? Just a few scorched hills…"

"That's ok, look at the scorched hills, at least you won't ruin your eyesight that way." She turned to her husband, "Slow down, my blood pressure's dropped and… What's so surprising about that? We're on these roads just about once a week."

"What are you trying to say?" His voice grew dry and kept his eyes on the road, but looked with his peripheral vision – his wife had pouted like an upset child. He smiled secretly – they had been together for seventeen years, a lot had changed in their relationship, they had both changed, but that pouty face remained the same. He grew warmer. He gave his wife's delicate fingers a slight squeeze, then put both hands on the steering wheel again. "I realize you're tired…"

"No, no," she tried to sound carefree, but it didn't work. "It's like I'm a criminal, but then I ask myself 'What did I do wrong?' I mean, he could consider…" she did not complete her sentence, sensing—rather than seeing—that her husband was giving her that look.

"Mom, what did the doctor say?" Their daughter broke the heavy silence, "Grandpa repeated today that he doesn't have much time left." She looked in the mirror – her father's face had grown dark. "Grandpa keeps saying the same thing, the doctor keeps shaking his head, and yet here we are every weekend – driving to the village, then driving back home… Could someone please tell me how long this is going to go on?"

"I can't even hope to take any time off, there's nobody else in my department at the moment," the man thought out loud, "Maybe I can take a few days of sick leave."

"Don't you need to bribe a doctor to get a medical report for sick leave?" The woman's voice was once again calm and lacking in emotion. "We have to pay back interest on that loan at the end of the month."

"Mom, what about my computer?"

"You'll have to wait till we've paid for the refrigerator…"

"So no computer for me this year either," the girl demonstratively raised the magazine to her eye level and leaf through it noisily.

"Maybe you can take some time off," the man asked without a question mark.

"No," the woman cut him off calmly. "There are going to be changes in the faculty, my life hasn't ended yet. At least, when it comes to my career."

"Since when were *you* so career-focused?" He realized that his joke sounded hollow.

"Since today," the woman's voice sounded metallic. "At least let me decide when I can take time off."

"You've always been the one who decides, and not just when it comes to time off."

"What are you trying to say?"

"Let's not continue this, shall we?"

"I thought I told you not to read," the mother turned around, "Didn't you hear me?" The girl didn't make a sound. "You're not even dignifying that with a response?" She said this in the same calm, emotionless voice, and then—so quickly that nobody realized what had happened—she grabbed the magazine from her daughter's hands, rolled it up and began to hit her in the face with it. "Perhaps you'll listen to me now? Cat got your tongue? Well? Say something!"

"Have you lost your mind?" The woman's face began to bleed from the slap that the man had given her – a tooth had lodged itself in her cheek.

The car slammed to a halt.

"Mom, are you all right?" the girl leaped forward, rubbing her stinging face.

"Get back in your seat," she said it in a way that froze her in place. "Give me a paper napkin," she took it from her husband and wiped the blood from her mouth. The napkin grew red. She carefully placed it beneath the windscreen. A second one grew red too. She put it next to the first one. Then a third. The bloody napkins were being lined up next to each other in such a ceremonious way they seemed to be the testimonies of a sacrifice of which only she was aware. Her husband and daughter watched, hypnotized. She stopped bleeding. She placed a fourth napkin, then turned to her husband.

"Why can't you force your father to leave his damn house and move to the city? I'm not like those other daughters-in-law. I'm not saying we should put him in a hospital or a retirement home. I'm saying let's bring him home and take care of him. What kind of life is this? Every weekend it's go to the village, come back to the city. Don't we have anything else to do? She's a kid, she wants to hang out with her friends at a café once in a while… What about me? You should think about yourself too – you're all skin and bone…" She grew silent, powerless. She gathered the paper napkins, crumpled them, and threw them out the window. "This is the last time. You can go and stay there for months if you want to, but don't force me to come with you, you understand? I'm not coming anymore."

"The doctor said he has two months left to live," the man examined the hands that had been overcome with a mild tremor. "Have patience, it's almost over." He turned the key in the ignition and transferred those trembling hands to the steering wheel.

"Right, so I'm heartless and I have no soul. Why don't you say that your father is just as much to blame…"

"Could you please be quiet?" the man almost requested.

"It's just him and his precious life…"

"I said be quiet!" He moaned, disgusted at the pitiful sound of his own voice.

"Mom, look! And he looks so relaxed lying there… there's a laid-back guy if there ever was one!"

"You want me to be quiet? What about the fact that your mother died because of him? She just gave up…"

"Dad, stop the car. It looks like this guy isn't asleep…"

"I said be quiet! You can stop coming to the village. You can forget my father if you want to, but don't stick your nose into my family's affairs."

"Mom, tell dad to stop the car… we're past him now… we need to go back. Mom…"

"Well, of course. I've been your wife for seventeen years, but I'm still not a part of your family."

"Shut up!" The girl screamed shrilly.

"What's gotten into you?" The father's eyes looking in the mirror saw an unfamiliar shadow.

"What are you shouting about? Your dad and I argue so rarely that now you…" the worse she felt about her own outburst, the less mercy the mother showed. "Don't you dare butt into our conversation. You were supposed to be reading your magazine now, remember?"

"What were you talking about? Who was lying where?" The father's eyes looking in the mirror had regained their usual color. "Well? What were you talking about?"

"Nothing," the girl puffed her lips and took on a terrifying resemblance to her mother. And when the silence grew so prolonged that it caused a sense of resignation, she flung out the words with a sense of near hate. "You weren't even near Grandma when she passed away. One day, you'll find Grandpa dead and shriveled in an empty home. And the weekends will be ours once again."

They did not speak until they got to the city. The car stopped at the first store. The girl gave her mother the magazine and smiled at her father in the mirror, rolling her eyes—a private joke between just the two of them— and stepped out. She wanted some juice. She stopped at the store entrance, turned around, smiled, waved her hands and stepped inside. Her parents waited in silence.

There was suddenly a commotion in the store – shots were fired, robbers shouted, someone cried uncontrollably… Days later, the shopkeeper—it was a miracle he had survived—would recall the last words of the girl holding the bottle of juice, "Why didn't you stop? What if that guy was still alive?"

* * *

"Stop near the village market," said the Brunette.

"I knew you were going to say that," the Blonde smirked.

"What can I say? Dried plums are my weakness…"

"It's not the only one."

They laughed. They were young, beautiful and confident. Very confident.

"We were lucky to finish early today," the Brunette knotted her ample, black, long hair at the back of her head with practiced movements, removed her light jacket, threw some chewing gum in her mouth, and stretched with satisfaction. "That gives me time to go to the beauty salon, my nails are a mess." She held out her manicured hands. "Do you want to come?"

"I don't think so," the Blonde lit a cigarette after a barely noticeable pause, "No," she said with a smile.

"Are you busy?" The Brunette was concentrating on examining her nails, and the question sounded almost indifferent.

"Not really…" she inhaled the smoke, effecting another pause, then asked, "Shouldn't we pop into the office?"

"Are you kidding? Go all the way to that place before tomorrow morning? Arrive in town a couple of hours early and use that time by going to the office? I wouldn't hold my breath if I were them…"

"Well, I'm going… a lot of work has piled up."

"Of course you're going. You're crazy about work. Perhaps if you'd said that a month ago, I might have believed you. But I'm not as stupid as you think I am, sweetheart." She looked over to her – the Blonde was driving the car like she was really enjoying it, while she had never managed to overcome her fear. *"You look so soft and harmless. And you behave so well at the office – polite, smart, a clean-cut mommy's girl… And you cleanly cut a path right to the boss' bed, didn't you, my dear?"*

"Why work so hard? Take some time out to have fun!" She stressed the word "fun" to reflect her bilious mood in recent weeks. "We'll tell the boss that we had a flat tire on the way and we got into town late."

"I'll tell the boss you had a strong headache and had to go home," she gave her friend a half-smile and extinguished her cigarette. "The material for tomorrow's presentation isn't ready yet."

"You know what? I really do feel a headache coming on." She laughed.

"Lucky you… My mother would've called this double luck – no brains and no worries! But she'd be wrong this time. Because with brains like that, you'll never have worries. Two years of sleeping with the boss on a regular basis and what do you get? You enjoy life any way you want. As for me…" She glanced over, the Brunette had closed her eyes. You'd be tricked to thinking she was asleep if not for the chewing gum popping in her mouth like gunshots… *"Interesting. What would she do if she found out I'd taken her place? I mean, the question of whose place I've taken is a relative one… I didn't have the brains that she did. All I did was sleep with him a couple of times and I ended up pregnant. Like an inexperienced little girl…"*

"Hey, we drove past the market," the Brunette put a hand on the steering wheel.

"Sorry, I was lost in thought," she put the car in reverse immediately, "Well, go on and buy what you need to."

"This is for the boss," the Brunette wrapped some dried fruits in a paper napkin and put it carefully in her bag. "I'll give it to him with his coffee tomorrow. He's crazy about it… like me," she looked straight into her friend's eyes.

"Really?" The Blonde stretched out the word without conviction, then hid behind her dark sunglasses and lowered her window. "*I'll tell him tomorrow… Why tomorrow? I'll tell him today. And I'll force him to take a decision. And we'll do things my way.*" She glanced over – the Brunette was chewing her gum with abandon. "*I wonder… did she ever get knocked up? Maybe she can't. I'm sure she'd love to get what she wanted by having his baby… Look at me, I've forgotten my own problems and I'm thinking about God knows what. So that's it, then. Today's the day… He said he's planned a romantic evening for me. Well honey, let's see what's left of that romance when you find out you're going to have a baby. If everything goes according to my plan, the first thing will be to drive this woman out of the office, she's really getting on my nerves now. The way she eats… the way she licks her fingers…*" "You're really eating those with relish! Give me some."

"I do everything with relish," the Brunette picked out a dried plum and held it out, "Even married men."

"There you go again…"

"I've never concealed any of it, honey." Was it just her, or did that last word sound like it was said with disgust?

"*Has she found out? We were careful, but she's the kind of person that would… Oh, you're getting fired for sure, honey—there, no less disgust on my part when I said that—ho-ney…*"

"Stop," the Brunette screamed, "I'm talking to you, can't you hear me?"

"Have you lost your mind?" She asked, after she had stopped the car.

"Look, do you see him? He's on the ground…"

"Where?" The Blonde was careful to conceal her short-sightedness.

"Up there on the elevated curb… he's lying there…"

"So what?" All she could see in the distance was an indistinct figure.

"Maybe something's happened."

"What could have happened? He's just a guy, relaxing." The hate that had accumulated inside her exploded. "You stick your nose into everything everyone does, I've had enough…" "*So she's been spying on me, that despicable bitch. She'd do anything.*"

"What's wrong with you? There's a guy lying in the sun there… Maybe he isn't feeling so good, maybe…"

"So many cars are driving by, you're the only one who wants to stop and help," she started the engine and they drove off, "A regular Mother Theresa…"

"Wait, I'm talking to you. Stop! Why couldn't we have just checked on him? I would've gone alone, if you didn't want…" Those last words were spoken in a monotonous voice, and she left her sentence unfinished as she examined the Blonde's unfamiliar face.

"What are you trying to prove? That you're kind-hearted? Why are you staring at me like that? Yes, I don't care! Someone out there has decided to lie down and stick his feet out – I don't care if he's asleep our dead, I have my own problems. Why should I help others, who's done that for me? I've got to where I am through my own resources, I haven't got my promotions by sleeping around with my bosses the way you have. Oh, what an angel…"

"Shut up, before you get me started…"

"What do you mean?" The Blonde turned fully towards the Brunette. "What are you going to say when you get started? You think I don't know that you've been spying on my every move? You know your time is up…"

"Watch the road… Oh, God… No!"

The Blonde managed to catch a glimpse of the car that was driving straight at her and slammed her foot down. A moment before she died, she realized she had hit the gas, not the brakes…

* * *

"With a price like that, it doesn't make a difference whether or not you sell the house. Why not keep it? At least it's a place you can escape to from the city heat in the summer," he took out a small bottle of juice from the refrigerator and held it out to the woman sitting behind him, "I don't know why I thought you might be thirsty." And he flashed a broad smile.

"I drink water when I'm thirsty, not juice," the woman said, but she took the bottle, wet with condensed droplets, and held it in her hands, realizing that her palms were burning.

"Your wife has not changed at all. She's still the same stubborn little goat," said the person sitting next to him.

"Stubborn, perhaps. But at her age, what do you mean by 'little goat'? She's a full-fledged nanny goat," her husband attempted a joke.

"For you, maybe," the woman looked unblinkingly at the mirror in front of her. She wasn't looking at the driver, she responded while seeming to look at herself.

The driver was her husband's childhood friend, gave the person sitting next to him a light punch and looked in the mirror.

"She wants me to repeat that his wife is the prettiest and the youngest thing. Well, she got what she wanted."

They drove in silence for a few kilometers.

"You're saying we should keep the house, but how? With what?" The woman seemed to be talking to the bottle. "It needs to be renovated, you need a car to come and go there. We can't bother you with that every time."

"I'm always prepared to do this for you guys. Like a boy scout." The driver's laughter echoed in the husband's silence.

"Disgust… That's all that's left in me – disgust. I'm disgusted by the brushes too, by the paint… I used to pick paint for hours, the guys would make fun of me… I would say that the smell of the paint tells me what I'm supposed to create. They'd guffaw. All the great painters were crazy. Great… Just a regular paint applier. He calls my wife stubborn. I'm the stubborn one, continuing this pointless endeavor of painting. Yes, I failed at life, while this guy… He was quick to get out of college and start his own business, so I need to ask him for favors all the time…"

"How's business?" He asked, knowing that every word his friend said would hurt and bruise his ego, demean him, reduce his own existence to nothingness in his own eyes and that of his wife. Yet again.

"Nothing to complain about, praise the Lord. It really surprises me, man. Everyone keeps complaining – there's no work, there's no money out there. But there's work and money just waiting for everyone, man! People just need to stop their useless talk and work a bit!"

"There's money waiting for people like you. And that fat-assed wife of yours is spending thousands of your money to have a figure half as good as mine. If only I had your body, she tells me as she eats caviar by the spoonful. It's crazy when she asks me what diet I'm on. If I tell her that on some days all we have

at home is bread and potatoes, she'd squeal with joy. I could slip past her to her husband if I wanted to… I can see the hungry eyes with which he looks at me. But that's not going to happen… I don't want that fat ass looking at me someday as someone who's eating her leftovers. Oh no, my dear businessman, I've found another way to get to you. You'll keep looking at me with those hungry eyes but you'll never have your fill. And the point isn't to maintain the honor of that weak rag sitting next to you. You need to learn that your money is useless if the woman in your sights is disgusted by you."

"Do you have any regular water?" The woman rolled down the window and threw out the bottle. "I want water."

A few minutes later, the car stopped at a small café on the road. The driver stepped out of the car and walked in.

"Were you really that thirsty? Or simply checking the effect of your charm yet again?"

"You know how he disgusts me," the woman responded calmly.

"Disgust…" the husband confirmed, "I know that feeling well."

He stepped out of the café holding a plastic plate full of apricots.

"The guy at the café said that these were good apricots," he said when they were driving, his eye on the road. "I said that they couldn't be good, because it was past the time of the first harvest. You know what that idiot said? 'That's ok, they might not be the first but they'll be your last.'"

"Yeah? Then what happened?" The man sitting next to him examined the apricots – that golden-yellow hue was his weakness.

"Nothing. I said a couple of things to him and he got the message."

"And then?"

"Man, the way that son of a bitch said the word 'last'…"

"I never knew you were superstitious. People like you don't need to believe in such things," the woman licked her sticky lips and smiled broadly. "You're meant to enjoy life."

"Life… what do you know about life? We're barely getting by, just about making ends meet every day, and then we're living with the fear that those ends can come loose anytime. You think I don't know why you dragged me here with you and brought me to this village? Your wife wants to sell me the house she inherited from her uncle, and what a price she's asking for it! They're starving with no food on the table, but they can't look you in the eyes and tell it straight. There he is, sitting next to me, the Picasso that wasn't… Oh, how he

used to pretend before! He would act like the next up-and-coming genius! But we saw how things turned out… And we see it now – barely selling one painting each year, that's how you work, isn't it? And your wife is no less of a pretender – acting like she's off limits. What a princess! She has no idea how many girls I go through every day, younger and prettier than her. What did she say – I'm meant to enjoy life? Yes, I am, I've still got a lot to get from life, so many loose ends to tie up… Who's that lying there? Is he asleep? Look at how relaxed he is, without a care in the world, stretching from north to south… I wonder if… could he be dead? Well, God bless your soul, then. That guy reminds me of that brat, he's really overdoing it. His behavior has been unacceptable lately. I have to tell the boys to bring him to me once I get to town… I have to drop these people home first… I mean, couldn't they get a cab once we're in town? I'd have to pay for the cab, of course, otherwise they'd have to go hungry till the end of the month…"

"This was such a good idea… With so much work to be done, we sometimes forget to just spend quality time together," he smiled broadly in the mirror. "We should get our families together someday." He looked at the man sitting next to him. "I'll try to find some free time and come to the studio. Maybe we can think of something…"

He stopped the car in the yard, stepped out and walked into the house. She could hear female chatter on the second floor – his wife had gathered her doppelgangers again. He slammed the door and stepped out. As he walked towards the garage, he noticed a shadow beneath the wall. Then the shadow stepped out and into the light – it was that brat. "Why you… I should've told the boys… You think you can beat me? Well, I'll show you…"

The last thing he saw was the barrel of the gun aiming at him. And he managed to think that when he falls, he should make sure his arms and legs are not stretched out in the same awkward way as that guy on the highway…

∗ ∗ ∗

The man on the curb stretched with pleasure once again, took a drag of the smell of the sunburnt soil into his nostrils, and sat up. The cars sped by below him and the monotonous buzzing of a water pump could be heard from the valley… He put on his socks, meticulously tied his shoelaces, and then hopped lightly to his feet. He had only been lying under the sun for ten minutes, but his face was already prickly. He would be dying of sunburn by nighttime, but a few minutes of carefree relaxation is worth that punishment. Before going uphill, he turned around. The cars below him sped past at insane speed, none of them concerned with him in any way…

1ˢᵗ of March

A Chronicle of That Day

THE CARPENTER'S NAME

He walked in and closed the door. On the other side of the door lay the street, the city, the Square that had been taken from him in recent days. On this side of the door lay his house – his property, created with his own hands and through suffering that only he had known. The corridor was in semi-darkness. He leaned on the door and took a deep breath, inhaling the smell—that special odor of his house—a mixture of the waxed floor, the flowers in the room, the kitchen, a barely traceable perfume, the sweat from his son's shoes stuffed between the wardrobe and the wall, and so much more. He did not switch on the light as usual. He knew that his face was barely recognizable – from the stress, the inhuman tension in his nerves, the powerlessness he felt that bordered on anger. He needed a brief moment to get himself together within and to rediscover the sense of calm that was always on his face… On the other side of the doors that led from the corridor to the other rooms, the everyday lives of his family members continued. His wife was in the kitchen – there, the cover of the pot slipped out of her hand but she managed to catch it so that only a dull sound could be heard. The sound of music was coming from his son's room – he was lost in his computer again while the Beatles sang about yesterday. He had given his son that album and he had been listening to nothing but the Beatles since that day. He smiled, or something similar to a smile appeared on his face for the first time in recent days. That half-smile hurt his face. He raised a hand to touch his face – ah yes, his muscles were tense, that was why it hurt.

There was silence in his daughter's room. She was lying on her stomach on the couch, buried in a book. All this belonged to him, this is the little world for which he lives, but a few hours later he would go back to the

Square, he would stand face to face with the other side and… He loosened his tie and switched on the light. He forced the person looking at him from the mirror to smooth the sharpened edges of his face, and he entered the kitchen.

"You're here? We'll eat in a minute," his wife walked up to him, embraced him lightly and looked at him questioningly. "How was your day?"

"The same as always," he managed to resist her stare.

"Yes…" his wife's 'yes' sounded so bland that, for the first time in eighteen years, he did not know whether it was a question, confirmation, or resigned understanding. "We'll eat in a minute."

Joseph walked into the bedroom, carefully hung his coat on the back of a chair and—it had already become a habit—ran his hand on the epaulette, counting the number of stars. He went to the bathroom. He washed up without looking in the mirror and stepped out onto the balcony – since the day his first child was born, he had never smoked inside the house. The sunset had a reddish hue, it was going to be a good day tomorrow… He strained his ears… no, the Square was far away, he could not hear anything. In the thickening fog, the Square was like an island in the distance – isolated, by itself, unreal… He threw away the remaining half of his cigarette and stepped inside.

On the table, there was a porcelain tray that grandma had left behind – they used it only to serve tolma. Next to it, there was a long-necked crystal carafe that was a memento from his mother – it contained a crimson wine. This belonged to him – the table, the carafe, which was placed on the table only at the beginning of the week and when they had company. This was also a tradition that their grandma had left them, along with the tray and the carafe. This was real – his family and this home that lived with the traditions of his forefathers.

"Dad? When did you get here?" the surprise in the voice of his sixteen-year-old son had a trace of puerile joy in it.

"Even if I storm into the house with a tank, would your computer let you notice that I'm home?"

"Tanks? Don't say anything about tanks," his wife seemed petrified for some reason, frozen helplessly in the middle of the room.

"What's wrong with you?" Joseph sat down without concealing his dissatisfaction, brought the carafe closer, and then smoothly slipped into a theatrical anger, "And don't you dare take the salt shaker to the kitchen – for the first time, we were going to have it on the table without having to remind you to bring it."

"What? The first time?" his wife was genuinely offended.

"Aram, wouldn't you agree with me on this one?"

"Come on, Mom, Dad was exaggerating," Aram waited for his mother to sit down while still holding on to the salt shaker, then he said, "This is only the second time."

"Well, now… at it again, are we?" his mother was powerless but angry, and she placed the salt shaker in the middle of the table with a strong sound. "This is, in fact, the *third* time!"

Joseph's heart grew warmer when he heard their laughter.

"Where's my Lusin?"

"Here I am," his daughter rushed in, walked up to him and hugged her father, then kissed him with a loud smack, "Oh Dad, if only you knew…"

"How much I missed you," her brother completed the sentence imitating her voice, then mocked her, "How original of you!"

"Love doesn't need to be original… That was well said on my part, right, Dad? Mom, I'm starving!"

Joseph picked up his glass and three pairs of eyes waited for the usual toast, "Thanks and glory to you, God!" But he was hesitating, as if he was seeing the living room for the first time, the room where they had celebrated his wedding and said goodbye to his parents for the last time. The hundred-something-year-old clock on the wall and his father's oak rocking chair seemed completely unfamiliar to his eyes. He looked at them one by one – his wife, son, daughter… They were his, they were the ones closest and dearest to him. His throat scratched with the bitterness of the past days and his eyes grew moist, the hand holding his glass began to tremble imperceptibly.

"May God help us… all," and he drank. And he was not surprised that his family understood. Joseph broke the heavy silence.

"Lusiné, what were you reading today?" He made no attempt at hiding how crazy he was for his daughter.

"I wasn't reading, I was writing."

"Poetry?" Aram dropped a gentle reminder about his presence.

"A school report," she managed to respond to her brother, stick out her tongue and make a face all at the same time.

"What's the topic? What's it about?" Joseph was enchanted by the beauty that was beginning to appear on his daughter.

"Responsibility. They've finally hired a decent literature teacher. Instead of memorizing the dates when authors were born and died, she's teaching the children how to think," his wife placed two tolmas on her son's plate as she spoke, he's a growing boy, after all.

"What do you mean?" Joseph looked carefully at his daughter, mentally noting that his wife knew everything—or almost everything—about their children.

"Well… what does responsibility mean? What literary figure can be examined as part of this topic? Rubbish like that," Lusiné took a few large gulps to down the apricot juice with a childish voraciousness, then she caught her breath. "But there's something else that interests me… I want to know…" she was gradually growing more excited and had forgotten about her food, tugging at her hair in her usual way. "When does responsibility become…" she searched for the word but couldn't find it. "When does it become something else?" In response to the three pairs of questioning eyes, she began to speak rapidly, "Well… when you start to do what you're supposed to… everything is done correctly…"

"Professionally," Aram said, supposedly to himself.

"Perhaps… But until when or where? Where's the limit?"

"Calm down, I've told you a thousand times. Don't rush into things," her mother poured her more juice. "Take a breath."

"What do you mean? Doesn't the word itself suggest the limit?" Joseph was surprised to feel the impatience with which he was anticipating his daughter's response.

"I was reading the Bible a little while ago, I was looking for…"

"Since when is she a believer?" Aram asked his mother.

"Let her speak," Joseph placed a hand on his son's. He turned to his daughter, "What were you looking for?"

"Dad, you know what the carpenter's name was? The one who made the cross for Christ?"

"His name? Does it matter?"

"I don't know… I was looking for it…"

"I've never thought of it, to be honest," her mother was pondering this, picking at the cabbage and meat with her fork. "Let's say it's Simon, or David… Luke or Isaiah…"

"Cain and Abel," Aram joined in.

"Matthew or Joseph…" her meticulousness as a teacher   was forcing her to remember, to go through the Biblical names she knew. She was taken aback by the laughter that had broken out. "What happened?"

"What was that you said, Mom? Joseph?" Lusiné smiled mischievously.

"Yes, what's wrong with that?" And then it hit her, and she looked at her husband guiltily. "Sorry…"

"What's wrong with what you said?" Joseph felt that the smile he was faking wasn't working. "First of all, you're only giving a possible name, and even if he was really named Joseph… Does that mean anything?" He tried to smile again to smooth over the silence, "Lusiné, are you going to finally finish what you were saying?"

"Well, if they've contracted him, and he's made a strong, durable cross, has he ever thought about how it's going to be used?"

"Yes… I never thought that my sister's pretty head was busy with such serious questions…"

"Let's try being quiet, shall we?" Aram finally shut up, though it was his father's look rather than his words which had this effect on him. "You go ahead," he tried to smile at his daughter again.

"Or what he thought when he found out that Christ has been crucified on the cross he had made."

"Do you have an answer?" Joseph glanced sideways at Aram.

"Only one," Aram's voice was harsh, bellicose. "It does not matter at all why he made the cross. He made a cross on which someone was going to be crucified – it could be anyone. And it would not be someone he knew."

"What do you think? You brought them up, didn't you?" he turned to his wife and gave a barely noticeable smile. Barely – one that only his wife could notice.

"Is that a compliment?"

"Nothing but a compliment," his eyes ran across his wife's face like an embrace, "The nameless carpenter… But why should he remain nameless? Let's say his name was truly Joseph…" He waited. They were quiet. "So, Joseph, who made tables, spoons and coffins, had to make a cross. And it had to be him, because Moses the blacksmith and Isaiah the mason could not do it. Nobody had the right to make that cross but he. He knew that, and that was the responsibility you were talking about. Any questions?"

"I'll get the coffee ready," his wife cut through the silence, "Lusiné, clear the table."

Joseph stepped out onto the balcony. It had grown dark, the silence was unusual. He thought that the perhaps the Square had gone silent as well, or perhaps the Square was like one of those islands that does not have a permanent location. It always wanders from sea to ocean and a little later, when he returned, he would find that it was gone…

"Dad?" He hadn't noticed Lusiné walk up, "Are you going back today as well?"

"Today as well, tomorrow too… As long as I have to," his voice sounded dry.

His daughter was going to say something, but the look in his eyes made her go back inside.

"Coffee's on the table," his wife's voice could be heard on the balcony.

He took a sip without tasting it. Aram was flicking through the television channels, on mute, the images rapidly replacing one another looked like an absurd movie.

"What's on your mind?" Joseph realized that this was the first time he was asking his son this question. He had grown. He only just realized that his son had grown.

"Our Luso is something else, isn't she?" He smiled with the self-satisfaction of a brother. "But I would have asked a different question…" He was choosing his words carefully, "Someone had given the order for the cross to be made, right? Didn't that person ever stop to think how Joseph would live with that decision? How he would live after he had carried it out?"

"Aram, perhaps you should shut up," the wife, who was placing the washed tray back into the cupboard sat weakly in front of Joseph at her son's final words.

"No, why should he?" Joseph did not look away from the cup, "We're having a good evening of questions and answers. All we need now is a question from you…" he looked squarely at his wife.

"When Joseph made the cross and got home from work, his wife must have asked, 'How was your day?' What did he say?" His wife managed to resist his stare.

"He said, 'The same as always,'" he pushed aside the coffee he had not managed to drink and got up, "Don't leave the house. Lock the door. Don't wait up for me, I have a key."

He walked into the bedroom, put on his jacket, and the stars on his epaulette twinkled in the mirror like harbingers of bad news.

"Be careful."

It had always surprised him—and sometimes impressed him—when his wife managed to silently appear at his side. This time, it was unpleasant. He did not want to talk.

"I had a dream last night…" she knew her husband couldn't stand it when she said those words. When they were younger, she had tried to tell him her dreams a couple of times. She had been mocked relentlessly, then the third or fourth time, after a difficult conversation, they had agreed that that idiotic sentence would never be heard again in their house. Joseph did not believe in dreams.

"And?" His voice was heavy with warning – stop now.

"I'm going to tell you about it," his wife walked up and looked straight at him. Joseph did not look away. "I saw them in the dream. They are unlike anything else. They will be in the city soon. In the Square."

"So what?"

"Don't go… at least tonight, don't go. Tonight in the Square…"

"Did you see that in your dream too?" He pushed his wife away from him and smirked bitterly, "I hope I didn't die… in your dream."

"No," her voice was barely audible, "Together with them, you were…" she had no breath left in her for the final word.

Lusiné was waiting in the corridor.

"Dad, let me remind you," her father had no idea what she was talking about, "It's March 1, the first day of spring tomorrow. Don't forget to bring violets for Mom."

"Thanks for reminding me, I had forgotten," he glanced at her conspiratorially, "And you will get your present too."

He turned around. His wife stood on the threshold, a suppressed scream on her tightened lips. He stepped out.

Joseph walked in and closed the door. On the other side of the door lay the Square – besieged, persecuted, annihilated, bathed in blood… He leaned on the door and tried to suppress the tremor in his hands, although he knew that he would never again be able to forget what he had seen and what had happened. The light came on. It was his wife…

And the carpenter's wife asked,

"How was your day?"

And the carpenter replied,

"The same as always…"

THE CITY OF ANGELS

When Luso the soothsayer—who wasn't really a soothsayer but someone with a wild imagination, living alone in a three-bedroom apartment in one of the best buildings on the large avenue, someone still expecting her life to amount to something, an "impressive lady" as she called herself—so when this Luso the soothsayer spoke before dawn to the man who sharpened knives and scissors that she had had a dream that night which was not just prophetic but something that was a hundred percent—no, a thousand percent!—sure to become reality, and when that man who sharpened knives and scissors relayed this word for word to Saten on the first floor—who did not have a single knife, much less a pair of scissors, to sharpen, but maintained, in her words, human contact with all layers of society—that was the moment when everyone claimed ownership of that dream. I don't know about the others, but I heard about that dream on the phone – I don't recall now who had told me about it, but it doesn't matter. What matters is that when I was being told about the dream on the phone, the television emitted a loud moaning sound, and the screen went black. And while I was trying to understand what had happened, the screen lit up again, the sound returned, and I relaxed. I was turning to face the screen when I heard Gohar's voice (yes, I remember now, it was Gohar who had called) exclaim with a groan, "Why did this stupid thing lose color?" I had not yet fully understood but then I saw it and grew anxious – my color TV was now showing images only in black and white. Without interrupting the conversation, I walked up to it and gave it a powerful thump on its top surface, and I heard it echo into the phone and then came Armine's voice (strangely enough, it was Armine at the other end now) complaining hopelessly, "It hasn't even been a couple of months since we bought it, what's wrong with this thing?" We came to the same conclusion, that the electric network must have caused this – they had probably cut off power somewhere and then restored it at such high voltage that it had damaged the TV tower. It was quite possible that our technical explanation had nothing to do with the real cause, but Anush and I (it was her voice at the other end of the phone at that moment) felt calmed by that thought, and we managed to get to the end of the dream without paying any further attention to the black-and-white screen that looked so unusual to our eyes. Luso, we all knew, was not really a soothsayer at all, but after living alone in her lavish apartment in the city center, when her husband took their son and went to the distant north to fully display his talent there for making money out of nothing, this Luso really went insane from that solitude within those four walls. And because she did not have the habit of visiting with her relatives, nor had she had the foresight to set aside a lover or even a potential candidate for such a "rainy day", all that was left to do was play the role of soothsayer for the residents of our building. And because the coffee she purchased was of the best quality, and the cups she brewed were the most aromatic, she soon managed to take on the reputation of someone who could decipher the passwords to women's secret thoughts in the grounds of the coffee they drank, an achievement that gave her peace. Her husband and son would send money every month and, at certain times of the day, there was no lack of people coming and going at her place, so Luso regained her mental balance, and one day became the full owner of all the secrets in our building, all our sins, old and new. And suddenly, that Luso, who was not a soothsayer at all, but rather the hoarder of secrets in our building, had gone and had a dream the previous night that ten angels had soared above the City Hall building at dawn for a few minutes before falling down with broken wings and bloodied bodies on the people. And when Luso had looked closely at them, she had realized that the angels had disappeared and, in their place… no, not humans, at least she had never until that moment seen such… even she did not know what those things were that she had not seen. And those don't-know-what-things had become to multiply right before Luso's terrified eyes – one turned into two, two turned into four, four into… And when she looked around, she saw that there were no people around her, the people had vanished, and she knew for sure that the buildings held no people, nor was there any movement or reflection in any of the windows.

And it was just those don't-know-what-things, that were unlike anything, which were quietly, multiplying though without movement, as if following orders of some kind…

I agreed with Astghik (it was Astghik she was talking to at the moment) that Luso was undergoing unpleasant age-related changes at the moment, and we both hung up at the same moment. I went to the kitchen but stopped halfway and returned. Luso (it was her voice in the phone now) said that she had tried to find out something about those she-doesn't-know-what-things-either in her dream, but one of them—just one—while splitting into two identical versions, had murmured a sentence, and when she had woken up with a scream of terror, the words "eleventh commandment" had throbbed in her ears like flowing blood.

I asked Luso (it was definitely her at the other end of the phone) why she was so scared now? It had been hours since her dream. She laughed hysterically and then it seemed like her sobs exploded in her throat and she gulped. "Is Aram home?" The phone went silent. "Will Aram… will Aram be at home? He hasn't been away from the Square for so many days," I muttered to myself.

It was two in the morning when he stumbled in and drank some tea without sitting down… Before he left, for some reason I don't understand, I gave him father's hat. For three years, I was trying to convince him to put on the hat at least in the evenings, when it was cold. He would refuse every time, coming up with some excuse – sometimes joking, more often angry. Last night, he took it and put it on, and I wasn't even surprised.

"I look like Dad in this hat," he smooched me on the cheek and left.

And I was wrapped in an unfamiliar serenity, as if his father was now by my son's side…

I looked around me, struck by my last thought. Quiet, it was quiet in the room, it was quiet in the building, I looked out the window – it was quiet. The television… was also quiet, black-and-white images were sparking out of it. But my eyes are used to the color and they could not make anything out – who were those people, where were they running, what was the ruck-us? I called my Aram on his cellphone. There was no sound. I looked at the telephone screen – it was also without color. Suddenly, I heard the sound of beating in my ears. At first, it seemed like my heartbeats were echoing, then the beats lost their rhythm and turned into noise, which then gradually turned into a monotonous metallic screech…

I stepped out onto the balcony – the yard was deserted. I tried to spot any movement or anyone's reflection in the windows of the building opposite, but all I could see was the cold impression of the windows. I came back in and my fingers, overcome by tremors, somehow managed to dial my son's number on my mobile phone. There was silence. The black-and-white on the screen had seemed to fade, the picture I knew so well had dissolved, but I could see some irregular movement in its depths.

I feverishly flipped through the TV channels. It was the same every-where – faded black-and-white figures were running this way and that, but because there was no sound, I didn't understand anything. I looked out into the street again – it seemed like nothing had changed, but… a few buildings away, someone appeared in front of a kiosk. And there were another two in front of the display window of that store. They were immobile and had not noticed me, but I withdrew instinctively. I did not want my eyes to meet theirs. Meanwhile, my fingers kept tapping and tapping on Aram's number, but he was quiet.

I threw a coat on and approached the door, but before I could put my hand on the knob, some kind of force pulled me back and brought me back to the window. There was the same silence on the street, but more of them had appeared, and they were not just on the sidewalks but also in the middle of the street. And it was only then I realized that the main street in the city had been empty – there had not been any cars, or pedestrians, the street… had died. As soon as I said this in my mind, that the street had died, my vision grew clearer and I saw the things that had appeared in the street seem to increase in number with alarming speed, or… were they splitting into clones?

I jumped away from the window, the television was in front of me. The screen was dark. My soul was burning with despair and I knew that if I thumped it on the top now, the screen would clear up and I would see what I knew had already happened and which had terrified me from the moment that Luso had mentioned her dream to the man who sharpened knives and scissors. I forced myself to raise my hand and slam that black box, which had blackened further. What appeared on the screen was not a light. The darkness dissipated for just a moment to reveal the ten angels, their wings broken and their bodies caked in blood, lying on the crimson pavement. In that instant, their faces were all branded into my soul one by one, and I knew that the tenth among them was my Aram, his hands holding the hat of his father, who had died three years ago.

The screen went black, never to light up again and I knew that it was them on the street – they weren't nothings-at-all, because the ten angels with their broken wings and caked blood had been dropped from the sky and now they were forced to split and multiply in order to finally silence the city with their transformation.

I walked up to the window – it was only them on the street. Unmoving and silent, isolated and condemned. But I knew that one of them—just one of them—would search and find me with its colorless eyes so that I—concealing my pain and desire for vengeance—could tell him about the eleventh commandment…

THE ELEVENTH COMMANDMENT

The Transition from life to death is so unexpectedly different that one willingly stops breathing and places oneself before the wind. And then comes the weightless joy – you are free! It's true that when you realize you've lost the concept of time you change a bit, but because you cannot tell when, at which moment exactly after the Transition you lost that time, you are approached by the distant voice of reconciliation and you are free for good…

"But not you…"

"Why do you say that?" I turned around. It was someone like me.

"You're still wearing your clothes from the other side," the glances at my blood-caked shirt were indecipherable.

"They haven't managed to… They'll give me new clothes now, or a bit later," I said and I regretted it. I knew the reply I was going to get.

"Yes, there is no time here, so there is no now and later, either. You should have received your clothes for this point of Transition…"

I looked at the clean and colorless clothes the person wore. I no longer felt the coldness of my shirt heavy with blood. I looked and could not see myself in those eyes.

* * *

I appeared before Him.

"You will go back," He said.

I felt with surprise that I did not want to. I did not want to return.

"The person who murdered you has not been punished there. Not by the living. And he will not be."

I was hurt. It was tactless to mention out loud that you had been killed. It's true that you moan countless time in pain before the Transition, "Why? Why? I want to live…" and a flood of tears pours from your eyes, and you manage to recall all your misfortunes and insults, you indiscriminately hate everyone who remains there, because they will continue to live…

You drown in sorrow. Perhaps life has dealt you many blows, but it should have spared you death… And suddenly, I saw my mother's face, she had not left me alone. She was walking up to me, in just another moment… she embraced me… Everything changed, now everyone was around me – those I loved, dedicated myself to, those I made happy and bitter… I loved those who remained here and I was happy that they were still alive… I had never been so full of love…

"I don't care," I was absolutely honest. "He wasn't punished there, he'll be punished here."

"No, he must bear his punishment there, among the living… The law of the Transition must not be violated."

The pause grew longer. He was waiting for me to speak. And I was forced to ask, "Am I the one who will punish him?"

"No. You will simply accompany the Other." His words tasted like lead, the lead that was still inside me. And I realized that some people are not free of pain even after the Transition.

* * *

[67]

I did not like the Other. Even before I had seen him, I knew that I existed for him only as long as the murderer had not been punished.

"If you think I'm going to help you… don't hold your breath," all I needed to do was lead him to the person that was my final memory, hidden behind a black mask. I knew that I had become the shadow of his most lucid dream.

"The feeling that has taken over you has no name, don't seek one in vain."

I liked his reply. And when life flowed between us without causing any pain, nothing was present on our faces. We were not present.

* * *

I had returned, but I had no place among the living. This did not surprise me. But when I found no place within me for the living, I cocooned myself within the feeling that had taken over me. And I saw from there how life flowed among the living, and the pain it had caused me received an explanation.

The Other had not seemed to notice me. He only tried once to bring me out of the cocoon formed by the feeling that had taken over me, when he suggested that we watch my murderer from a distance.

"Can I see anyone else besides him?" Like, my mother, for example? She's alone now in our empty apartment," I asked the question I had prepared in advance in what was almost an amiable voice.

"No," he said at once, and I realized that he had been waiting for that question.

"Then I don't want to watch him, even from a distance," I smiled.

I am convinced that the Other had also been waiting for this smile.

"He will be punished whether you watch him or not."

And he was gone. He did not appear again until the evening news showed the body of my murderer, partly reduced to ashes. "An accident," the news anchor said.

At that moment, I saw my face in the Other's eyes. It was just like it had been a moment before I was murdered. And I managed to confess to myself that after the Transition, all I had been seeking was my face and my name – Aram.

"You fulfilled His commandment," said the Other, and I watched as my shirt, heavy with dried blood, transformed into a clean, colorless garment.

"Which one? I thought He had issued ten commandments."

"On this side of life, there is only one commandment – the eleventh."

Somewhere far away, life continues to flow, but I managed to absorb a bit of the pain it caused me, leaving that bit of joy more in the days of those who continued to live. I know now that, in the sky above my city, the angels soar free.

BEFORE THE ECLIPSE

"Impossible… you're talking nonsense! An eclipse? An eclipse… when, where, and by whom was that made up and spread around? And today of all days! Pick up the calendar, will you? It's on the right side of the table… open it to today's date… found it? Now read what it says."

"April… today's date… sunrise is at… past 7… sunset… Next page, "Born on this day"… A thought for the day… that's all. No wait, there's a joke at the bottom, do you want me to read it?"

"You're a joke… I'm telling you to try and find the word 'eclipse' there. Does it say eclipse? Is it a solar eclipse or a lunar eclipse?"

"All I've heard is that it's an eclipse."

"Well, then, find the part where it talks about the eclipse and read it out."

"How can I find it, it's not there!"

"Well, if it's not there…" he forced himself to grit his teeth and calm his voice. "Scientists know in advance—years in advance, not months!—when and where the next eclipse can be seen, and all that information is always provided everywhere, even in stupid calendars like this one. Get it?"

"Got it, but…"

"No, you didn't get it. People don't find out about an eclipse an hour in advance."

"Two hours and six minutes…"

"You still don't get it. There isn't going to be an eclipse today…"

"Now there's exactly two hours to go…"

"And we still don't know if it's a solar or a lunar eclipse?"

"Maybe it's a stellar eclipse."

"Get out!"

It was like the wind wiped the assistant away. The door closed noiselessly.

He caught his breath, got up and walked to the window.

On the other side of the bulletproof glass, it was a serene and calm morning. The blue from the cloudless sky descended on the city, the air would ring out if one could touch it. From his elevation, the city was almost in the palm of his hand. He held out his hand, felt the weight of the city in his palm, but did not tremble – he was ready, he had long been prepared for that weight. Sliding his eyes across that familiar panorama of the city, he noticed that the fog which had appeared on the Square a few days ago was now thick as a shadow. He turned around and went back to his desk, feeling behind his back how the calmed city was floating in blue tranquility. Except for the Square. He sat down and checked the day on the calendar – his assistant had not missed anything. He smiled secretly, read the joke of the day and pushed the calendar away. He felt with surprise that his heart had grown heavier, as if the weight in his hand had moved to his heart for a moment. What foolishness… it was just nerves. In the silence of the massive office, he began to quietly count the seconds, the minutes… One hour and fifty minutes to go.

The barely audible knock on the door hinted at who was behind it. He straightened his shoulders and leaned back in his chair. The uncommunicative face of the assistant that entered was a mask, he owed his rapid ascent in this building to that mask. He came closer and stopped at the very distance from the desk that matched his perception of official appropriateness. And, as always, his unblinking eyes stared at a point that only he could determine.

"What's up?" He asked, more than indifferent.

"You already know – an eclipse."

"In the world?" he tried to smirk as stingingly as possible.

"In the city," did the bland voice echo in the room, or was it his imagination?

"Or perhaps on one street in particular?" he felt like he must have smiled kindly.

"At the Square," the assistant was looking in the direction of the window, but he knew that the shadow that had grown heavy on the Square could be seen by him. Only by him.

"Is everything ready?" He put an end to the unspoken words in a voice that did not accept any objections.

"Perhaps we should postpone it?" He heard anxiety in the bland voice, and also fear…

"Do you expect me to believe that what you discovered two hours ago is an eclipse?"

"Two hours and six minutes ago." Was that doubt which had grown in the bland voice, or fear?

"Two hours and six minutes ago even," he can bear the weight of the city resting in his palm, why should he not be able to bear what these people were saying? "You believe what you're saying, while I…" a brief pause was necessary to emphasize the importance of his words, "I have to think about the safety of my city."

"You've already thought about it," the assistant's bland voice grew confident, "The decision to postpone the swearing-in ceremony will be announced in a few minutes through all our news channels…"

"What?" He had not wanted it to, but the scream flew out of his throat and slammed itself from wall to wall in the massive office. "What?" he repeated, barely audibly, then he flew from his place and walked to the window.

On the other side of the window, the city floated in the blue that had been calmed by his will and persistence, and its weight pleasantly tickled his palm. He held out his hand and the city obediently settled into it. Slowly, very slowly, he balled his hand into a fist and brought it up to his eyes. It was quiet inside, the spring air ringing. He did not look in the direction of the Square – it was just the shadow grown heavy on it that was not willing to obey him.

"Post-pone?" he broke the word up into its syllables, "Never! Everything will take place as I have said it – point by point, second by second…"

"But…"

"But, for the safety of my city…" the pause lasted until the point when the opaque mask of the other person seemed to transform. Perhaps insignificantly, but it transformed. "Nobody should step into the street, even to buy food. They should stay at home, behind closed doors, sitting in front of the television. Go and tell all the news channels to announce that my swearing-in ceremony will take place without the city." He was unable to hide his self-satisfied smile – the other person had forgotten about his mask and was blinking rapidly.

"Your order will be fulfilled, sir," and he left the room, repeating as if to memorize the phrase, "The city will not participate in the ceremony… the city will not participate…"

He opened the door, his palm was sweaty, covered in cold, viscid droplets. One paper towel after the other ended up in the trash can but his palm was not dry. The dials of the clock approached the expected hour. He covered his palm with the last paper towel remaining in the box and closed his fingers tightly. It was almost noon.

* * *

When the assistant entered the room, he was putting his signature on the final document.

"Your decision has been executed. The city is forbidden from participating in the swearing-in ceremony. The rest will take place exactly as planned," the assistant's trained voice reported while his eyes examined with surprise the white edges of the paper towel peering through the fingers of the fist of the man to whom he was speaking.

"I'll be right there," he snapped through gritted teeth as he tightened his fingers further and walked to the window.

"You have exactly five minutes," his assistant reminded him from behind and shut the door noiselessly. Only he could close doors that way.

Nothing had changed on the other side of the window, not even the shadow that hung heavy over the Square. He turned around and waited for the dials to count down the final seconds… he stepped out. His footsteps echoed dully in the silent, deserted corridor. They went up and down the stairs, and the halls passed the barely audible creaking of their doors to each other. He realized with some delay that the clocks hanging on the walls were showing different times…

There was a long and seemingly endless motorcade of black cars at the main entrance. The impenetrable mask worn by the assistant standing at the armored vehicle opened its door. They sat in the back seat, next to each other. The motorcade slowly crawled through the fenced walls. He closed his eyes – he did not want to see the funereal profile of the person sitting next to him. And only a muffled, and then a clearly audible noise forced him to open his eyes and pull back the black curtain on the window.

"What's this?" the scream that escaped his throat shattered the bulletproof glass. "Who allowed this?"

The person sitting next to him pulled back the curtain on his side unhurriedly and looked out.

"The streets are deserted, as you ordered. There are no people, no vehicles. There are law enforcers standing at the necessary places…but they are nothings-at-all… don't pay any attention to them."

"How can I not pay attention to them?" he managed to lower his voice. "Why have people filled the streets? Who has allowed them?"

"They don't even look like statues… they're just… I wouldn't get angry over them," the person sitting next to him drew the curtain again and leaned back in his seat.

"I don't care about that eclipse that never happened and never will! I had ordered that the city would not participate… Hadn't I said that?"

"They are good in their service. The best thing is that they multiply by splitting into clones…"

"Send them all home right now! I don't want to see another one of them," he was no longer trying to keep his voice calm, it was like a screech.

The voices of the people on the other side of the hermetic window could not be heard, there were only mouths opening and closing on all the faces. He was unable to look at any of them in the eye.

"But their biggest advantage is that these nothings-at-all are deaf and mute, also blind. That is why they are ready to do anything for you… even… I can't say what…" the person next to him was mumbling absently. He realized that his companion was not listening to him and looked at the back of the driver's head. He spotted the driver's absent gaze in the mirror. He finally grew conscious of the pain in his clenched fist – the fragments of paper towel that had slipped through his fingers had turned slightly pink.

The motorcade's route passed through all the streets and alleys of the city, even going into the dead-ends. And the people that had filled the streets, alleys and dead-ends were coming and going like alarming waves. He noticed that every time they took a turn, the number of cars in the motorcade went down, as if the street-alley-dead-ends were swallowing them up. The more the motorcade's length decreased, the closer the eclipse's breath, the less power his orders had, even the very latest one he had signed. The weight of the city, which seemed to have resigned itself to remaining in his palm, seemed to grow more and more unfamiliar, while the shadow that had covered the Square came closer and closer…

The person sitting next to him had buried himself in the leather cushion of his seat in such a way that he was barely visible. The back of the driver's head demonstrated a lack of readiness to be a part of what was to happen next, and the last car accompanying them in the motorcade disappeared in the roundabout near the Square.

The solitary car screeched to a halt in front of the Square. He knew that the person sitting next to him would not step out of the car, but he looked over his shoulder. Just in case. He was alone. Even without having seen it, he knew that the Square was also packed, and alarming waves of people were rocking this way and that; he would have to elbow his way through the crowd if he wanted to get to the center. The paper napkin he had squeezed in his palm grew moist again. He tried to open it but his fingers did not obey – the shreds of paper appearing through the gaps in his fingers were almost reddish. Breaking through this wall of people, every step he took, was becoming impossible, but he knew that he had to reach the platform in the middle and stand on it. There were just minutes till the ceremony was due to begin, the hurriedly assembled platform appeared before him… Just a few more steps… A little more… Yes, he was going up… There, he was at the top! And the city was below him, the city that seemed to have submitted to his hand. And only the shadow hanging heavy on the Square—this disobedient Square—had isolated everyone without discrimination, from him to the most elderly of flower sellers, so that his silent and therefore most dangerous memory ruminates in this enforced separation… Now he was here, at the very top, and he could calmly unfold his balled fist and his palm would also be able to bear the Square's weight.

The ringing of the clock declaring noon sliced through the air. The blackened shadow menacingly gathered and thickened on the platform, at the top of the high pillars of the Opera building. He took a deep breath and opened his palm wide.

The bloodied, transparent paper napkin, that now resembled a plastic bag, rose up to meet the falling shadow…

The eclipse had not yet begun.

He was already in the city.

2008-2009

The Seventh Day

It was the wrong day for me. It was not my day. It was my heart… it was beating slowly.

Sitting at an open-air café and shifting my indifferent gaze, hidden behind dark sunglasses, from top to bottom, meaning from the sky to the tiled floor, I did not know yet that twenty-one years later, on a hot summer day like this one, I would say these words in this order, with this particular emphasis, and would feel cold under the shawl cast across my shoulders.

And it was not that my mind was tired and my body was spent, but the fact that I would say those words in that order, with that particular emphasis, and the random people who were around me would understand nothing, but would most certainly be awed by those words, because the last words of someone leaving this world always seem important for those who are still living. Especially when they remain unexplained.

* * *

Seated at the open-air café, I shift my indifferent gaze, hidden behind dark sunglasses, from top to bottom, meaning from the sky to the tiled floor. I enjoy the inebriating heat of August that had come and filled the space beneath my skin, clogging all my pores, becoming a kind of second skin and undulating with small ripples, forcing the acknowledgment of the presence of my own body at every moment as an abstract observer, a secondary being.

"Am I late again?" The man sitting in the chair opposite pulled the ashtray towards him in a habitual movement, placed his cigarette pack and lighter next to it, and only then looked at Her.

"I don't know," She hadn't wanted it, but the response had already been voiced with its total indifference. "I was enjoying the sun." Perhaps that would mollify what She had said?

"Yes… you're enjoying the sun and it's enjoying you," a slightly twisted smile appeared on the man's face. "As always, I'm not a part of it."

"The last thing I need in this heat is the need to allay your fears," She did not regret saying it.

"Which are not completely baseless," he said it as if to make sure that he said something, but the lighter in the man's hand seemed to have grown smaller, as if it had split into two halves.

"Don't start. I've brought a new piece," a business-like tone appeared in Her voice, "Read it."

"With the right of first night?" Like every time, the man held out a hand and waited.

"No. This time… you weren't in town," She was surprised. Why did She have to explain Herself?

"Five days," the man clarified, just in case.

"Whatever," She took out a bunch of handwritten papers and straightened the edges with clumsily calculated moves, then held out the pile to the hand the man had extended.

"How many people have read it?" He was in no hurry to pick up the papers.

"One. Just one," the dark sunglasses did not reveal Her eyes – had they grown darker?

"If only at least ten people had read it," the man was not looking at the dark sunglasses, but he knew that Her eyes had grown darker behind them. That was what happened when She felt guilty about something, and then angry about feeling guilty. "Give it to me, I'm forced to be the second," and he placed the papers tidily on the table, as he always did.

"You could also have been the tenth."

"Or the hundredth. That is neither good nor bad. It's just the order in which things happen." Like every time, the man was convinced that he had lost a part of Her this time as well. And he thought that he had not reconciled himself with that fact. But he was surviving.

"You won't forget me, will you?" he asked like every time, and expected the same reply – "I'll forget you."

"I don't know," She said, and Her voice had never sounded truer.

"Let's get married," the man said in an attempt to verify something, or perhaps as a way to keep up the usual game, and he expected the same reply – "It's kind of late today."

"Let's," She said and got up from her place, "We're meeting tomorrow, aren't we? I'll come after six."

And She left.

The man, who was waiting for six in the evening the following day—and only he knew how much he was waiting for it—watched Her leave and thought that women leave men much earlier than necessary and before a final explanation. Today was that day.

* * *

She stepped out into the street. Standing on the sidewalk, She felt the man's eyes on her back. She thought that the gaze following Her consisted mostly of contempt. Nothing else was possible when a woman was leaving. She was leaving first.

She crossed the street, as always, at the intersection, under a green light. She walked unhurriedly. The sidewalk was on the shaded part of the street, She felt cold. A flash of interest appeared on the face of the woman coming from the opposite direction. She realized that She was not the cause of it… it was her smile, that spread from ear to ear and shone stunningly, sprinkled with a set of teeth right out of Hollywood. She added an unsuppressed laugh to the smile and—to herself—the thought that She was going to another meeting without having finished the first one.

The shiver came and went through her body like a tickle – it was the sun. As the years went by, Her dependence on it increased. For some time now, She had convinced herself that only it was able to heat Her up. Not warm her, but heat Her up—the toes of Her feet, Her nose, the nipples on Her breasts and Her thighs—only the sun.

She saw Him in the distance. He was sitting at the back of the table they were just at in the café, in a similar chair, and the ashtray on the table is the same. The cigarette is, too. Only the lighter is different. And the chuckle that was still rolling about in her mind stopped with this thought.

"Am I late again?" She asked and felt bad. She had not wanted to start that way.

"I don't know," He glanced at her quickly and then looked away.

"Sorry," She said – it was a word she was used to, it came to the rescue.

"You shouldn't be the one saying sorry to me. You shouldn't be saying sorry to anyone," He looked like a grumpy boy.

A forgotten corner of Her heart warmed. But when she realized that she did not know what to respond, she was quiet. She was forced to be quiet.

"Here, you can write with this," and He placed an elongated box on the table.

She grew thorny inside. Again?

"You know I don't like it…"

"It's just a pen," He wasn't even trying to hide His misunderstood surprise.

"I don't like receiving gifts."

"This… isn't a gift. You're going to write with it."

Thornier still, She picked up the box and felt an unexpected warmth in Her palm. Was it the pen? Upset by this thought, she nearly flung the box on the table, but on Her half of it, not His.

"I was seeking you and I found you," these words were followed by silence.

"What can I say?" She thought, "You came when it was no longer possible to change anything."

"I'm a strong person. I've always been able to leave when I've wanted to. But now…" the words came and then silence.

And then He was talking about something and She caught herself thinking that she was growing familiar with alarming rapidity to his words and his thoughts, which often gave way to each other and turned into a powerful flood, as powerful as He was, with manly—manly enough to cause shortness of breath—force that would double in His silence.

"I don't believe it," these four words came by themselves and settled down within Her, grew comfortable, and took over Her thoughts.

"I don't believe it," She wanted to say out loud and see how He would respond. She could not. Those four words that had risen and reached her lips and were about to escape at any moment, received the signal to return, and they descended falteringly, settled down deeper, and began to weave their web of doubt.

"You're not looking at me. Your eyes, which are open to everyone, do not care for me. Where are your eyes?"

"It's time for me to go," She said and thought that this one, who had appeared unexpectedly and had swept the others aside immediately, would leave just as powerfully. And the gaze… the gaze would have everything except contempt.

She left the garden. She felt His eyes on Her back. She thought that the gaze consisted mostly of… tenderness. She was not surprised. There was still time for contempt. Very little—perhaps an insignificant amount—but there was still time.

It's my heart… it's beating slowly. I think it's the seventh day…

I like the hospital room – one of its walls is made of glass and I can look for hours at the sky, which can only be that pure and hot in August. An unfamiliar serenity has overcome me – I'm so grateful—but I don't know to whom or what—that my final day and my final hour will come this month. There's an absurd flowerpot on the window sill with roses that are absurdly beautiful and I know that my final gaze will fall on those flowers, then rise up to the sky and remain there.

My heart is barely beating, it sometimes just constricts painfully, and I am grateful to it too. That will be the last thing I feel – pain. I mean, it couldn't happen any other way. Whenever I made any decisions, I always trusted it, and the more painfully it constricted, the more certain I was that I was making the right choice. Although I found out that, on each occasion, I had killed a portion of the happiness in my heart.

The cashmere shawl wrapped around my shoulders is like congealed blood on the white bed. Damn it, it was just like yesterday when, in a small southern town in a foreign country, my eyes had searched in an old-smelling shop and found that shawl. My eyes were perhaps very eloquent, because the elderly Frenchwoman picked it up, stepped out from behind the counter, and placed it on my shoulders. Our gaze met for an instant, and then we closed our eyes with a habitual smile. It had remained, almost forgotten, in a corner of the lowest level in my chest of drawers for so many years even though it had established its presence in my room immediately from the moment I had taken that shawl out of my suitcase and flung it on my bed after my return. And it had only been once that I had tried to cover my nakedness with it, in front of the only man for whom my body had been created… And, hours later, I carefully folded and wrapped in wax paper the cloth that held the memory of His hands and His body, knowing well that I would use it to cover myself on the most important day of my life, so that my solitude would be denied its final victory and would be unable to take my memory from me, which will accompany my gaze to that final blue August sky. And my solitude, which I had worn like a blouse for decades, was going to retreat in those final moments, because my shawl would have kept the memory of His hands and His body as faithfully as a dog in its knots, its color and folds, so that it can serve it up to me as a final consolation.

∗ ∗ ∗

"I don't believe it. I do NOT believe it!"

She thought she had said it to herself, but the co-worker at the next table raised his head and glanced over questioningly, while the girl lazily working at her computer arched her eyebrows, "What *your* problem?"

She stepped out into the corridor, walked up to a window and put her forehead against the glass. "So I said it out loud. That was all I needed – thinking out loud… That's enough. That is all!" She turned around sharply, return to the room, sat down and pretended to continue working.

"Are you feeling okay?" the girl leaning over Her table and examined Her face carefully.

"Why, do I look bad?" it was a phrase She was used to, it came to the rescue.

"You look the same as always, but your eyes…" the head leaning over the table clicked its tongue thoughtfully.

"It's nothing, it'll pass," Her response came out quite carefree, She was happy with how her voice sounded.

The head closed its eyes and leaned on the table for good. The girl hiding behind the computer raised her eyebrows further, "If I feel bad a thousand times a day, I'd still want nobody to notice…"

She jumped at the sound of the ringing phone. The girl picked up the phone, looked at Her and saw that her eyes had grown darker. "Now who is she angry at?" She laughed to herself, "Hey, it's for you," she put a special emphasis on the last word.

"I'm not here," She said and ran out the room, escaping from her fluttering heart, fleeing the questions she was asking herself and her powerless anger…

He wasn't supposed to come. He did not have the right to come. He came and ruined everything. He came unexpectedly, so unexpectedly that She didn't even recall how he had come in the first time, what he had said, how he had managed to find the reason for his next visit and leave it as collateral, and then come the next time with an excuse to come several times more. And then he would come because it would be surprising if he didn't. And one day She felt that he was all around her, that he had swept away everything else, and not even the devil—her own devil—knew where her previous life had been swept aside and moved.

In her dream, she was alone, smaller, standing and waiting, frightened and obedient.

He was coming from afar, frightening and commanding, and he…

She jumped, and half an hour later she was still telling herself that it was only a dream, a stupid dream, and there was no He next to her, that there was nothing in the dark, lonely room besides her, it was the shadow of the moon creeping in from the window above her head, it was not Him smiling, his eyes closed.

In the morning, she opened the lowest level of her chest of drawers and took out the shawl she had sought and found in the old-smelling shop of a small southern town in a foreign country, and she put it in her bag.

"The best way to be liberated from a man is to sleep with him," she said out loud. She didn't care if the room heard her. And she left.

*　*　*

The silence lazily comes and goes in my hospital room, like a reflection of high tide and low tide in my mind. The nurse that enters only when one procedure or the other is necessary, and the doctor that comes in even less frequently, are sincerely indifferent to the point of moving me. They do not hide the fact that I am fading away, that my heartbeats are stubbornly growing fainter and the emptiness between them is filling with the silence in the room.

They caress my fingers—perhaps it's only in my head—or the folds of my shawl and I suddenly notice that it does not have the same color as before, it has faded. The unexpected fear born within me forces me to bring the shawl closer to my face and smell it. No, the memory of his body has been absorbed by ever stitch of the fabric like a faithful dog, and I sigh with relief, for the first time in the last few days.

A barely audible sound attracts my attention to the window sill – one of the rose petals has fallen, it was the sound of its death. A minute later, the second petal is not there either – it slides downwards obediently… I turn my eyes to the heavens. No matter how serene you are, it is not easy to see the shadow of your own death.

I die a second time. Perhaps that is the reason that I don't have that animal fear that—I am convinced—lies dormant in each of us, waiting for its time. This one is calm, it is going to take me with it. And I will keep Him within me as final payback, then simply follow my death.

It was difficult the first time, when after dying I had been forced to live like nothing had happened the next day, and all the innumerable and countless days that followed…

*　*　*

The most difficult thing is to turn a sensation into words. At least for me.

When I was going to Him, there was none of the inhibition or even fear that comes with a first date, I had even lost the emotion that is common in such a situation. I did not feel the impatient expectation within me to love and be loved. My heart, which was beating the same way it always did—regularly and even sleepily—was saying nothing to my thoughts, which were hovering irregularly like sparrows pretending to be asleep, estranged from me. I was going to a man for the first and last time in my life in order to be liberated from him. And He forced me to go to Him this way, to strangle the razor-sharp pleasure of submission, to kill the joy His love was giving, to close my eyes so as not to see the face that was more familiar to me than time. He had gone mad with love, he loved his own love, he loved me and the way I kept repeating to myself, "The end… the end… this is the end…"

I was saying "the end" when my lips were blooming in his, I was whispering about "the end" when, inch by inch, he made my body into his, I was

[82]

sobbing "the end" when my constantly alert mind went numb because He turned his sensation into words. He was perfect, and love had never been so full of harmony and joy for me.

All I had to do was give him up. Because staying there would end in loss. Because, from the first touch of His hands, I knew that all I needed was those hands, that only his breath could save me and that I had to see Him every day, every hour and second… He had to be mine, only mine, I could no longer share or split Him with anyone else.

And so I said, "The end."

* * *

She entered the room. She had been absent for a few hours but it felt like days had gone by. The objects and items seemed unfamiliar, she even looked around and it seemed to her that she had entered another room. She took off her shoes and coiled up on the couch. She was looking at the window and the evening on the other side, which turned into night, then grew pale and dawned. When she rose from her place, she screamed; her body had gone numb and dead, her legs had been unable to hold her up. She crashed into the couch and woke up to the blood flowing within her; she moved, shifting thousands of fine needles under her skin. She rose from her place again, took out the cashmere shawl from her bag, wrapped it up in the wax paper she had brought from the kitchen and put it in the lowest level of her chest of drawers. After that, she tried for a long time to stop the tremor in her hands. She thought that this was perhaps how people tremble when they dig graves in a cemetery for the first time.

She turned on the shower but sensed that she did not want to get under the water. She could not. She turned off the water, leaned against the wall and tried to persuade herself – what happened? Hurry up, the day had begun a long time ago! She had to turn the faucet, but her hand would not obey. Her back to the wall, she slowly slid and collapsed on the floor, then noiselessly, dully wept.

She did not know when it happened, but she managed to get up, stand beneath the shower and turn the faucet. The hot—nearly boiling—water poured down on her with a happy hiss. She stood beneath the water for a long time, powerless and desperate, until the last shadow of his love had been swept off her body. She turned the water off and remained standing there. How long? She did not know. Until her body was dry. She could not touch herself. She had always been scared and disgusted by dead bodies.

* * *

It was a bad day for me. It was not my day. It was my heart… it was beating slowly. It was the seventh day…

It was summer, August. My August. The shameless heat of which had penetrated my skin on so many occasions, beating in sync with the rhythm of my body and forced me to submit to the sun. Twenty-one years ago, perhaps on this very day, I was enjoying the sun, enjoying it while fully dominating it. And then one of the people came who had been fated to accompany part of my life, and I lost the sun. I left some time later, the same way I had left before and then I felt his eyes on my back… And I don't remember what was in that gaze, what dominated. I mean, it is such a secondary thing, something to which you should never pay attention. I realized that so late…

Then I went to another park, I remember how I was irrepressibly chuckling in my mind on the way… What was I laughing at? With God as my witness, I don't remember… but what a good chuckle it was! How crazy and good I was…

I saw Him in the distance. I don't remember now what I was thinking or feeling that day, but today, on this hot August day of mine, which no longer warms me (and neither does the cashmere shawl on my shoulders), I can see everything so clearly—the park, myself, the chuckle coming and going in my mind, and Him…

He had come. He had come to find me. And I knew that He had found me the way that I had found Him. But then… what happened then… Four words came by themselves and settled down within me, grew comfortable, and took over my thoughts. "I don't believe it." Whom don't I believe? On that faraway day, I thought I did not believe Him. But later, much later, I confessed that I did not believe myself. I was saying those four words to myself, because His love was real and strong, but I… had been afraid to love for a long time. And I would never be able to pay for His love with mine. I tried to liberate myself, to run away – I went to simply sleep with him. But I lost.

Because I understood in a few hours that I could not live without Him. But I could not live with Him either. And so I said, "The end." My heart is beating slowly… ever so slowly. That had happened once twenty-one years ago when, coming back after seeing Him, I wrapped in wax paper the cashmere shawl that I had used in an attempt to cover my nakedness from the man of my life, but I only managed to confess to myself years later that this was not why I had bought the item I had sought and found in a foreign country. I cleaned his body with that shawl—his powerful and lovely body, covered with love juice and sweat—with the tenderness that had been born in my fingers but had never been there before, cleaned it like the most miserly of scrooges worrying over his wealth, such that I would not lose even a drop of his sweat, not a crystal of love juice. I cleaned it with a sense of ownership for the first time – that sweat, that love juice were mine, only mine, and giving them up would be the same as dying…

They say that a person's heart functions normally for six days, and the beats grow slower on the seventh day, the heart rests. My heart lived that way for only one day, twenty-one years ago, when I gave Him up. And now, this is my second, and final, Seventh Day.

The rose petals crashed onto the window sill with a powerful noise. The last one would soon fall, but I wouldn't see it… Random people pour into my room, I cannot see their faces and don't want to. My hands clutch at the shawl and I know that I will say the words now that I first thought of twenty-one years ago, sitting in an open-air café, my indifferent gaze hidden by a pair of black sunglasses. And just a moment before the rescuing darkness I understood that I would say nothing, it was pointless. The last words of someone leaving this world are so unimportant… especially when they remain unexplained.

The Drowned

"When he was going to the river for a swim and kept embracing and kissing everyone he met on the road, why didn't any of them stop him halfway and turn him back? Why didn't anyone try to say something in an attempt to change his mind, huh? Didn't they see that he was drunk? Didn't they see the coldness in his eyes when they let him go – go, swim in the waters melting in the spring… And now they're burying him. Oh, how they're burying him! I would be envious if this had been something worthy of envy." It was the Woman of the House, her voice full of righteousness, her movements – lordly, her anger – obvious, her doubt and fear – knotted in her heart.

None of the people in the room watched how she rubbed sand into the sides of the kettles, polishing them shamelessly and casting them aside. She wasn't arranging the kettles in the cupboard, she was throwing them aside so that they would strike the floor noisily and she wasn't even casting a side glance to see how the smooth copper sides were wrinkling when they fell.

"And now their hearts ache, don't they? They pretend to be grieving and inconsolable, as if they can't come to terms with what has happened. But what has happened will only last for a few days as material for their conversations and gossip. And why are they walking past our street? Why is it *our* street that they have to walk past? They could find another way around, couldn't they, as if ignoring us, or scared of us, or who knows what? What other reason could they come up with to forget the street on which we live? But no, they have to go out of their way to come specifically to this street so that they can find some loot to feed their dirty fantasies, forgetting the coffin they're holding above their heads. But they won't find what they're looking for on this street, will they?"

There were three people in the room, three women. The day stood outside the room, set aside for something specific, something that had not yet begun. Each of the three sheltered behind their unspoken thoughts, and had already interpreted the thing that had not yet begun; they were serene on the outside, but were mentally looking forward to the exciting joy of mortal combat.

"What they are seeking is not in the street!" Her dried fingers poked about the tobacco, pinched out some and arranged it in the paper, then adroitly wrapped it into a cigarette. A moment later, her furrowed face disappeared in the stinging smoke. She was the Mother of the House. Her voice was bent, her movements were broken, her calm was false, her knowledge and expectations were knotted in her eyes. "All they need to do is cross the street. Close your balcony door, put the key on a chain, and hang that chain from your neck, if you can't safeguard your house without a lock."

"Yes, I'm a dog, I'm the kind of dog that barks but doesn't bite. You won't forget that if anyone will. But I am also yours, your flesh and blood, why am I to blame if you cannot remember that? At least once in a while," the voice of the Woman of the House bent in that moment.

"There's so much to forget before I remember that… at least once in a while," the voice of the Mother of the House coiled out of the stinging smoke.

"Yes, you can't do that for sure. And I will stay where I am, a dog that barks but doesn't bite. But I'm not to blame for not having a chain." The Woman of the House had used up and emptied the water in the pot and was now arranging the scattered kettles in the cupboard. "What is a chain, after all? After all these years, I've ended up not even deserving of one."

"This is the day that makes you worthy of one," her dry fingers pulled out the tarnished silver from the folds of her black dress, a chain with large links that hung in the air like the bearer of bad news, "Here! All that remains is the key."

The shiny black sparks in her eyes now demonstratively calmed, the Woman of the House plucked the chain from the protruding, talon-like fingers of the Mother of the House, and put it on her neck.

"The key will come too," she promised through pressed lips.

Outside the room, where the day stood, an undetermined noise could be heard. The Mother of the House looked expectantly at the Woman of the House and the Woman of the House cast a lordly look at the third person in the room.

The third person, who was the Wife of the House, recoiled in her place.

"Not yet," she said, "They're still far away. They will take a long route, they will stop at three places, and only then… they're still far away."

The silence of the three was unbearable. The silence of each one was heavy by itself and oppressive, but one could bear it. But the silence of the three women intertwined was enough to make the room explode. Outside the room, the day was just beginning.

The garden door slammed loudly. The room sighed with relief – the door would open now and, albeit for a short time, the trebled silence in the room would retreat before the Man of the House.

"Are you waiting for them?" he examined the silence of the three from the threshold.

The three women, trapped in their unspoken thoughts and the events that were about to unfold, hid behind their dropped eyelids.

"Did you know about today, is that why you were using that tarnished silver chain on your prayer beads lately?" the Man of the House asked the Mother of the House with a grandchild's voice.

"Do you think you'll be able to twist this key in a rusted lock? You had to oil the lock in time, at least once a week, to be able to use the key now," the Man of the House said to the Woman of the House with a son's voice.

"I don't want to see you on the balcony today. It's not a big thing to ask of you, so I'm not asking. I'm ordering it. Don't step outside the room!" The Man of the House said to the Wife of the House with a husband's voice and then softly, so that only she could hear, "Please."

He said it and smiled bitterly. He could imagine nothing more amusing than being the only Man of the House.

Then, at some point, time lost him and he was plucked out of where he was and flown to another location.

The Mother of the House took her century-old prayer beads with the shiny stones and began to mumble words to the Lord's Prayer nobody else could understand.

The Woman of the House picked up the bottle of oil from the sewing machine and used her trembling hands to pour some into the opening of the lock on the balcony door, then going through dozens of keys, keychain by keychain in order to find the one she needed.

The Wife of the House closed her eyes and saw the approaching procession which carried the swaying coffin in front of it like a glove used to declare a challenge. And she saw him lying in the coffin, his clothes drenched, his hair wet, the space between his teeth and the wrinkles of his mouth containing sand, his throat holding the final scream that never managed to escape.

The Man took out the bottle from the cupboard, poured the vodka in a large glass and gulped in down. His face did not change its expression, he did not have shortness of breath, he did not wipe his burning mouth with his palm. He tasted the tear flowing inside his eye with the tip of his tongue and was frozen by its bitterness.

"What was he trying to say? That he was going, and he would remain in the water? What was he trying to say, what…"

"Don't blame yourself for this," the Woman of the House stood up, "That is what he would've wanted – for you to seek someone to blame and then pick yourself. I won't allow it. Is that why I brought you into this world, all alone and against the rest of the world and its people, for you to go and take on the burden for someone else's guilt today? Anyone would have done the same in your place. A woman born for love is a man's to claim. I raised you by myself, but I raised you a man. Don't blame yourself!"

"He couldn't even if he wanted to," the voice of the Mother of the House exploded, "When you brought him into this world by yourself—all alone and against the rest of the world and its people—did you blame yourself?"

"Why would I blame myself?" the Woman of the House frothed, "I was a woman born for love and I found my man. I found him and I said – you're mine. What business is it of mine whom he belonged to before me? I said you're mine and he became mine."

"Yes, he did, but…" did the Mother of the House smirk, or sob?

"Yes, he did, but… then he went to the flooding waters and remained there. And I did not shed a single tear. Whose eyes were supposed to watch my tears? They said she has a heart of stone, a witch with a shriveled soul, but I had no need to weep before the world, my tears were within me, they were mine. Yes, he gave himself up to the water, but he did not leave me empty before the world, his son was in my womb…"

The Wife of the House felt a coldness in her palms.

A word had remained in the corners of the mouth of the drowned. It was the same word in both corners, which had turned into a wrinkle and twisted the mouth into an unrecognizable shape. The procession had come closer, she was running out of time to understand the wrinkled word. And she had to understand it for sure. The Wife of the House shut her ears tightly, the conversation in the room was not allowing her to concentrate. She had to find the word, pluck it from the wrinkle.

"I've seen this talk and argument from the first day I opened my eyes. And I haven't understood any of it to this day," the Man of the House mocked, "But you could have at least spared us today, couldn't you? You could have avoided going back to your story."

"She can't avoid it because she can't forgive me for being left all alone and against the rest of the world and its people," the Woman of the House said, tired.

The eyes of the Mother of the House sparked with the bearing of bad news, and she ensconced herself in her silence.

"I'm sick of you," the Man of the House said with sudden disgust, "She can't forgive…" he looked at his mother with a filial bond. "It's not you she can't forgive, it's her… her! Haven't you understood after all this time that you are simply a copy of her?"

"And you are a copy of me," the Woman of the House grew angry, then mellowed in the hardened silence. "Now that we've said everything we wanted to say to each other, has anything changed?"

The Wife of the House shivered – the drowned was wet, drenched. It was strange. Hadn't they fished him out of the water two days ago? The old women had bathed him, dressed him in soft and dry clothes, dried his disobedient hair and combed it. That same disobedient hair that would pop through the spaces between her girlish fingers and shine in the light. Two days ago, it had transformed into a compliant hairstyle under the cold fingers of the old women. So why was he wet and drenched again on his final journey, when the sun was blazing down, why was water dripping and dripping from his hair, gathering in the cavities of his closed eyes and disappearing under his eyelids?

"He should never have left, supposedly to see the world or pretending to be seeking something out there… He should have taken the woman born for his love to his home, put seven locks on the door, and then gone to find whatever he was seeking. But no! He believed that she had to wait for him, that she would wait until he returned one day. Why did he get up and leave? Didn't he know that there were other people in the world besides him who would definitely take the woman born for his love?" The Man of the House joked powerlessly, emptied the bottle and flung it on the balcony. "I don't regret it. She's my wife, even if she wasn't born for me. He should never have left… And now that he's gone and drowned, what was on his mind? Who can say?"

"Go and lie down, you need some sleep," the Mother of the House grated.

"No," the Woman of the House cut in, "My son is no coward. Why shouldn't he be there? He has neither stolen, nor plundered. He has claimed what was coming to him."

"If only I felt that you believed what you were saying. If only I could feel that – I would die with a clear conscience," the Mother of the House offered a drop of compassion from her watery eyes.

"From what I can see, you still have a long life to live," the Woman of the House smirked bitterly, then turned to her son, "Go. Your place is there. Go and join the rest. Along the way, take the coffin at its heaviest end and bear its weight more than the others do. Let them see that you're a man and that you fear neither the stares of others, nor the weight of the coffin."

The Man walked up to the Wife of the House, who has hiding behind her closed eyes and ears.

"Look at me," his voice contained more threat that he had intended. He tried to soften it, he should not show how afraid he was. "Listen to me. Don't step out onto the balcony. Whoever calls out to you, whatever they say – remember me. It's just one day – you hold out, and it'll be over. Got that?"

The Wife of the House looked at him with the eyes of someone who would not return. It was as if the large pieces of ice mixed with the water had poured into her heart with a loud hiss. The Man of the House felt cold, unbearably cold, and looked miserably at his wife. Then he stepped outside silently. And the Wife of the House saw in her mind how he blended into the crowd of the procession, approached the coffin sideways and brought his shoulder up to it. Nothing changed on the face of the drowned, but the water started dripping more rapidly.

When the procession was one street away, the prayer beads of the Mother of the House came apart and hundreds of little stones crashed to the floor with a clatter, rushing to the garden. The legs of the Mother of the House went after them despite herself, while she kept turning back and trying to say something. She could not. Her legs were too stubborn and she disappeared in the shadows of the trees.

The fingers of the Woman of the House, trembling with haste, were trying to fit the last two keys left in the bunch into the lock. When the last one slipped in and did not budge, she angrily threw the bunch aside and tried to remember. Her eyes grew dark with the effort and hissing blood rushed to her ears… And she remembered that many years ago, she had put the key she was now fruitlessly seeking into one of the drawers beneath the sewing machine. She recalled this and trembled – would she manage to find it in the other room and bring it in time? Before leaving, she walked up to the Wife of the House.

"It's just a few minutes. You'll hold out, and then it'll be over. Hang on until I'm back. I must close the balcony door and put the key on the chain." The lordly Woman of the House had never been this meek and defeated. "It's no coincidence that I deserved to receive this chain on this of all days. I must be able to bring back that cursed key in time…" She realized that the Wife of the House could not hear her. She could not hear anybody. She pushed aside the panic that had engulfed her and went for her last resort. "One should not look at the face of a drowned man who was thirsty for love, punished by love, and overcome by love. You should not look at it because it contains his final gaze, hidden beneath his eyelids, and his final words, concealed in the corners of his sand-covered mouth. And, on his final journey, he is seeking the one who will look and say…" she went quiet in horror, but it was too late.

The eyes of the Wife of House had returned from where they had gone. The Woman of the House, who had wanted to frighten the Wife of the House with the story she had just made up on the spot had forgotten that she still believed in stories. She realized she was defeated, she knew that the only salvation now was to find the key. And she flung herself out of the room.

The Wife of the House looked at the emptied room and smiled.

Footsteps were approaching. There was no noise, no chatter. Only footsteps that were approaching the house with a threatening shuffle.

The Wife of the House stepped out onto the balcony and looked at the coffin swaying above the people's heads.

The Mother of the House, breathless in her meaningless search for the stones, crumpled on her weakened legs.

The Woman of the House, finally holding the shiny key that had been found in the depths of a drawer, opened her hand and saw that she was in fact clutching a rusty piece of metal, and she collapsed weakly to the floor.

The Man of the House, heaving under the heaviest corner of the coffin, closed his eyes.

The drowned man slowly opened his eyes and smiled. The face of the woman who was born for his love lit up. Even if he was in a coffin, that was the face of the man she loved, and the smile she knew so well, kind and loving as always. The wrinkled corners of the drowned man's face smoothed and the word came to life.

"Come," said the drowned.

Did the woman born for his love hesitate for a moment, or was it the life behind her that was trying to hold her back? Even if it were so, it did not succeed. Because the foot of the Wife of the House stepped on the empty bottle and it exploded. The wave of the explosion embraced her, lifted her up and threw her against the pavement below, in front of the coffin. None of the hundreds of people saw anything, or even heard the final word that had escaped the drowned man's throat as it went and cuddled with the lifeless body of the woman born for his love.

The Black Bed

When I found out about its existence, it did not surprise me, because I did not know then that I could experience surprise. But it did frighten me, because I already knew about the existence of fear. The world was a closed space in those days which would sometimes open and broaden a little with each discovery I made. Until I found out about its existence, I had burned my fingers with the steam curling up from a boiling teapot and that painful constriction revealed to me the stranger located on the left side of my chest, fluttering inside me, clenching and relaxing with the waves of pain writhing through my hand. That was how I found out where my heart was located and, before going to sleep, I would stuff my head under a pillow and hear it beating as it echoed in my ears under the warm and dark cushion. I had also discovered the hazards of height – I had climbed up the back of the couch and then crashed to the floor on my head. After that, in parallel to my long, monotonous sobs, I tried to relive those few seconds in which I had been flying… until I had struck the floor. So I was five years old and almost adjusted to the world around me when I discovered its existence.

That evening, my parents had gone to the theater with our neighbors—the parents of Anette and Aren who lived on our right, and those of the twin sisters Mané and Nané, who lived to our left—while we—the youngest, Aren, three years old; the oldest, Anette, eight; the twins, six years old; my brother, seven, and me, five years old—were at Anette's place. Why had we gathered at Anette's house? That was how she kept a tight hold of us so that no harm would come to any of us, nor to the furniture in the house, and so the adults would manage to take a break from us for at least a few hours once a week, while lauding Anette and heaping praise on her in return. She pulled out all the stops when it came to using her efforts and imagination to keep us busy, and we worshiped her and obeyed the way that only children can worship and obey. When and how that talent of hers turned into a black and dark power… And it was much later that I realized this was so, when it was no longer possible to turn things around.

But let us go back to that evening. My mother was simultaneously knotting my father's tie, combing my brother's curly hair and stuffing a bag of raisin pie into my hands when she repeated yet again,

"You will behave yourselves… Listen to Anette. In any case, I'll find out from her if either of you don't do what she says…"

"I don't want to," my brother surprised me; he had always been the first to rush out the door and run to the neighbor's house.

"What?" my mother asked, absently looking in the mirror to check the pattern on her socks.

"I won't go!" My brother's voice sounded more confident.

"Oh, by the way," my mother recalled and reached to the top of the cupboard to bring down a new box with a model airplane. "Anette will help you assemble it."

"I don't want Anette!" my brother repeated stubbornly.

My mother turned to me but I managed to look away in time.

"Lilo, what's going on?"

But my father held my brother with one arm, took the box with the other, and stepped outside. I followed them out and, when my mother slammed the door unexpectedly, I wondered if it would ever open the way it did before, silently and with an open heart.

"The show's probably over by now," Anette looked at her watch as she finished reading us the story.

"Can we look out the window?" the twins got up at the same time.

"I want some water," my brother said as he put the assembled plane on the table and stood up.

"I want to run around," Aren leaped up from his place.

"And I want to show you all something," Anette's smile transformed into something else.

"What?" we asked, almost in unison, except my brother who remained silent.

"I'll tell you what it is if you stay in your places, otherwise each of you wants to do a different thing," Anette said, seeming not to have noticed the suspicious look my brother was giving her.

Everyone obeyed her and sat down. I had been sitting all that time, and got up.

"Where to?" Anette asked in a stricter voice.

"I want some water, I want to run around and look out the window," I went on the offensive, not knowing why.

"Oh, is that so?" I thought that Anette enjoyed my response, which had been a surprise even to me, to be honest. "You can do what you want to, and I'll show them what I had in mind…"

I did not hear the rest. I drank some water in the kitchen and it seemed warm and unpleasant to me. I looked out the window and saw nothing, because the kitchen window looked out to the wall of the parking lot, and when I returned, the living room was empty. Voices were coming from the corridor. I stepped out, they had gathered around a green door. I knew that that was Anette's grandmother's bedroom. That winter, they had put her in a box and taken her away when she had been sleeping, and Aren had later said that she had gone very far away, to the end of the Earth.

"Why did you come here?" Anette made no secret of the fact that she wanted to hurt me. I had not known at the time that there was hurt in the world.

"I'll go right away, but only if my brother comes too," this was the first time I was making a decision for my brother.

"No, your brother must definitely stay," Anette sneered and pushed my brother towards the door. "Will you enter?" My brother recoiled at the question.

"He isn't going to enter anywhere," this was the first time I was so brazen, and I liked it a lot.

"There's something beneath Grandma's bed," Aren jumped into the conversation, "Anette says that it's always been there, and that it starting coming out after Grandma left…"

"Shut your mouth!" Anette silenced him only after he had said everything, and then she turned to my brother. "If you're not a coward, you will go in and walk up to the bed," she drilled her black eyes into my brother's, as if I were not even in the room.

I could not make head or tail of this, but something seemed to tell me that I had to go against Anette at that moment, the love I had felt for her previously was transforming with alarming rapidity into a feeling I could not name. I suddenly realized the terror that had overcome my brother and my body was covered in goosebumps, as if a bucket of cold water had been poured over me. As incredible as it seems, I was reading his thoughts at that moment, "I'm scared… but I'll walk up to the bed… and then what?" I saw my brother's heart shrinking, as if Anette had grabbed it and was squeezing. And I realized that our own door would never open the way it did before, silently and with an open heart. I pushed everyone aside, opened the door and walked inside. The heavy brocade curtain had left a narrow crack of window uncovered, and the shine of the full moon from the window as well as the light from the corridor visible through the door slit were enough to see the bed. The broad, brown, oak bed, which had a cover that reached the floor. The room was heavy with a strange smell. Anette peeked in from the door slit and laughed,

"Don't you want to move?"

I took a first step, then a second and a third… Then my shoe touched the bedcover. And the door closed. My eyes got used to the semi-darkness and I decided to count to five and then step outside. At that very moment, I felt that there was something under the bed, it was slowly approaching the bedcover. My heartbeats grew louder, much louder. So much louder that the thing under the bed must have heard it, because it crawled or slid to the bedcover, and then something dark came up to me… I don't remember how I flew out of the room and threw myself to the floor in the corridor, while someone else had recollections of seeing the twins sobbing, Aren's whole body trembling, my brother trying to unclench his rigid fingers, as Anette carefully locked the door and put the key in her pocket.

* * *

When my parents walked in, talking and laughing loudly, we were sitting on the couch and listening to another story by Anette. None of us every spoke about what had happened, not that evening, not ever. We had forced an agreement of silence on each other, because our acute children's intuition had suggested that this was the only way to be safe. I understood later that there would be no salvation for two of us, because I managed to resist Anette, but Aren could not help but submit to the power of the game Anette and I had started.

[97]

"Congratulations, at least you'll be free of this madhouse for a week," Sona from the news section said to me as soon as I walked in. "Like I always say, the boss has a thing for you…" She pretended to have simply been thinking out loud as she took a large gulp of coffee.

"If the boss had a thing for me, he would have approved my vacation days," I turned on the computer while simultaneously tossing my cap at the coat hanger; I did not miss.

"This is no less of a vacation. We're going to be here covering the dirt of the election campaign, while you're going to write about a library celebrating its hundredth anniversary in a peaceful hillside town."

"Hillside… peaceful?" I hissed, my eyes on the cap still swinging on the coat hanger. "Wallowing in this muddy election doesn't seem to have dulled your taste for finding sensational news stories…" And suddenly, I was alert like an animal sensing danger. "What do you mean? What library?"

"If I'm not mistaken, that God-forsaken little corner is your birthplace," Sona stated thoughtfully, her eyes turned to the ceiling. "It's both a business trip and a visit to your birthplace… Oh no, the boss isn't even trying to hide that he has a thing for you…"

I began to sink in pungent, rotten-smelling waters and I felt like my throat was constricting and would not open again. I barely managed to grab my bottle of pills from my bag and rush to the restroom. I was there a long time, trying to banish the only desire that had enveloped me – to lift my feet off the ground, curl up on the windowsill and wait until the dark thing that was approaching would crawl away from me…

*　*　*

"Yes, of course… We read your articles and we're proud that our town has produced one of the famous people out there in the world," the owner of the hotel was registering my details with savage rapidity and spewing out her words just as quickly. "Your parents… how are they? I remember them, yes… they were a handsome couple…"

"They live with my brother on the other side of the planet. Raising their grandchildren," I tried to smile.

"Yes, of course… And you?" the elderly lady's eyes were full of words.

"I'm by myself for now. The good thing about 'for now' is that it can last forever," I hoped the lady would appreciate my humor.

"Yes, of course…" judging by the expression on her face, the lady did not appreciate it. "Do you remember the twin sisters?"

"Mané and Nané."

"Yes, of course!" the woman was almost sincerely happy. "They both have twins, can you imagine? Mané has twin girls, Nané…"

"Has twin boys," I muttered.

"Yes, of course… Nature's mysteries, don't you agree?"

"More than you know," I smiled enigmatically. "Now, about the library… who's the director?" I asked, although I knew the answer well, I had found out back at the editorial office.

"Anette, you probably remember her." Was it just me, or had something unfamiliar crept into the woman's voice?

"Yes, of course!" I repeated in exactly the same way as the woman had been saying, and then I added, to mollify her, "You could say she's a childhood friend. And Aren…"

"Yes, of course…" she cut me midway and was surprised, "You didn't know?"

"Didn't know what?"

"He died."

"But he must have been so young… what happened?" I could clearly see Aren in my head the way he had been that evening, his whole body trembling.

"I don't know. There were some rumors about it in town back then, but I've forgotten," the woman closed her register with a doubtful noise, gave me a key and tried to go back to her previous tone of voice, "Would you like breakfast in bed?"

"Yes, of course!" This time, we were unable to keep ourselves from chuckling.

The room was clean and comfortable, but seemed slightly old. I quickly emptied my suitcase and stood under the shower for forty minutes, and then started to pace aimlessly in the room, trying to stretch out the time until I had to walk up to the bed. Then I held my breath and stood a meter away from the bed. Then I was able to force myself to jump on the bed and wait, frozen like that, until my heart calmed down and I could close my eyes and get under the covers, convinced that I had managed yet again to save myself from the thing that was crawling up to me from under the bed.

I am past thirty, a confident and—without false modesty—beautiful woman. More than a dozen men have wanted to sleep with me. I've rejected them all. With no explanation. And if I were to explain… that ever since I was five years old I have been unable to walk up to a bed, whether during daytime or at night, whether at home or in a new hotel… And that someone else's presence… I mean, what would a man think if he saw a woman with a face twisted in fear, jumping onto the bed from a meter away?

Anette welcomed me with a warm smile, aromatic coffee, and home-made cake. I had sent her a message in advance, asking her to make a list of the rare books and archived documents they held. We interrupted our coffee drinking to exchange meaningless words, and then she accompanied me to a kerchief-sized room, half of which was occupied by an oak cupboard with many shelves, covered in books and papers, which later turned out to be locked with no key in sight. On the windowsill, there was the coffee maker, a cup, and a can of coffee.

"This is a great setting for work," I examined the books and said, more as a way to avoid silence, "I can see that the library is in good hands."

"You wanted to say something else," she said indifferently.

"Yes, of course!" I laughed mentally at those three words that obsessively kept coming up. "Your parents…"

"Preferred the retirement home."

"Yes, naturally…" I was not surprised, "And you…"

"I'm alone, but I wouldn't say it's only 'for now.'"

"I guess that works," the cover of the book I was holding was at least one hundred years old and this was a justifiable reason to avoid looking at Anette.

"You wanted to say something else," she said stubbornly.

"Or rather, to *ask*," I looked straight in her eyes.

"So ask," she openly sneered, but did not look away.

"Why did Aren die?"

"Did he have a choice?" She walked up to the window to avoid looking at me, and I noticed how her body had grown old and dry.

"You forced him," I said very softly, hoping that she would not hear.

"At first, I thought the same thing that you did."

"The owner of the hotel was uncomfortable when this topic came up."

"She doesn't have the brains to think about it," her disdain exploded through her words.

"How did it happen?" I asked, more softly.

"I don't know. I always kept the key. He had gone into the room at night. He did not come for breakfast in the morning. Mother said that his bed had not been slept in. We ran to Grandma's bedroom. He was so small and helpless on that bed. We kept his coffin closed at the funeral." My skin seemed to feel how she ended each sentence with a period – a dry and hopeless period.

"Why was it closed?" I could not help but ask.

"His face was unrecognizable… twisted. As if he had seen something he was not supposed to see," she turned sharply and faced me. "It was supposed to be your brother instead of Aren. If only you hadn't interfered that day…"

Before I knew it, I was by her side and the bulging artery in her throat was throbbing against my hands, which were squeezing it.

"I saved my brother, but you failed to do that," I hissed, strangling the desire within me to suffocate her.

I forced myself to release her, then pushed her away and did not turn, until I heard the slam of the closing door.

We managed to avoid meeting for five days. I would go into my room every morning, work till noon, then walk around town till evening, trying in vain to breathe life into my memories, which should really not have been so limited. After all, I lived in that city for eighteen years. But there was nothing I could remember, nothing except that evening. It was like the rest had never happened.

On the last day, I handed the books and documents to the library storeroom employee, the girl with the pleasant smile, who kept trying to remind me of her sister, whom I had definitely known, only received a guilty smile from me in response. How could I remember her sister? She had not been with us that evening.

After lunch, I packed my suitcase, sent my text to the editorial office, and felt so free that I was short of breath. I left the hotel and walked the streets aimlessly like I had the previous days. The weather changed unexpectedly, it grew cloudy and twilight descended upon the city sooner than its time. I had decided to go to a church, but the weather also changed my mood, and so I decided to return to the hotel and try to get some sleep – I had to be up early in the morning. I turned to take quick steps to the hotel and when I thought I was supposed to be close, I realized that I was standing in front of Anette's house. The dark windows stared out at me. I was sure that Anette was not home, but I was just as certain that the door would be open when I took a step and approached it.

Nothing inside had changed – the furniture, wallpaper, and the pictures staring at me from the walls had not even faded slightly or grown old. Standing in the living room, I tried to discern the outlines of the various items when I saw my brother's plane sitting on a shelf. My throat constricted – how good it was that he was far away from here, with no thoughts of ever coming back. All that surrounded me was the silence, but the corridor called out to me – I felt like our voices were still there. Confident, without touching the furniture and objects in my path in the darkness, I stepped toward the green door. The house was waiting for each step of mine, for each sign, for each movement of my hand. I knew that the expectation in these walls had stretched for so long, long enough to transform into a threat. And I was going to face that threat, I had no other choice. The same silence hung behind the green door and, as soon as I entered, I was struck by the air, heavy with a strange smell, the memory of which I had never managed to erase from my nostrils. The heavy brocade curtain left a narrow crack of window uncovered, but clouds covered the sky. The streetlamp was just as effective as the full moon had been when it came to lighting the room, where every object and every centimeter had been branded into my eyes. I walked slowly up to the bed, but my feet froze a meter away and refuse to step forward. I saw that something had changed in the room, but I was not surprised that it was the color of the bed. It had gone from brown to a dull black. I tried to move forward but in vain. I was held back by that one meter, which had become my guarantee of staying alive through the night and greeting a new day. And from that distance of one meter, I saw how

the thing under the bed came to life and started to crawl to the bedcover…
The nightmare was happening again, but I knew that if I could jump onto
the bed from this one-meter distance, I was safe. My body grew tense, my
muscles clenched, the instinct of awoke within me of a hunter out to catch
prey in order to avoid becoming prey. I had to make yet another jump from
death to life. But my eyes fell on the black bed, which was growing blacker
and blacker, shining with rays reflected from the streetlamp.

I knew that Anette was waiting in one of the corners of the library. I
knew that the fingers of her parents, drinking milk before going to bed at
the retirement home, suddenly went numb, dropping two glasses on the
cold tiled floor and shattering them. I know that the twin sisters felt the
irrepressible need at that moment to burst into tears and, ashamed at that
display, would conceal it beneath an uncontrolled roar of laughter. I knew
that my father and mother were praying in church for their daughter, who
forever remained a mystery to them. I knew that my brother was parched
and wanted water, but could not unclench his spasmed fingers. But I had
no way back. Every night since that evening long ago, I had been pushing
away the thing that was crawling towards me from beneath the covers. From
the age of five to that day, I did not know what it meant to walk to the bed
with my eyes open and sit down, then slowly raise my legs, lie down and
go to sleep. Or to turn to the man waiting for you in bed and think about
anything and everything except the thing waiting for you beneath the bed,
the nature of which you never managed to comprehend from the age of five
to this moment. So I walked up to the blackened bed, sat on its edge and
forgot that my feet existed.

Anette will be in for a surprise in the morning. My face will be so calm
and bright that there will be no need for a closed coffin.

At the editorial office, they'll be a bit surprised when they see just a
headline—The Black Bed—followed by three pages of drawn lines, instead
of the article they expected. But that will not take long, the next muddy
political scandal will show up, and it will sweep away the title of the only
story I had written.

20 July 2011

Turnabout

I don't want to wake up. I'm awake. I don't want to leave my bed. I'm already in the bathroom, brushing my teeth. And although I know well that I don't want to leave the house, I'm walking down the street, shaved and in a fresh shirt. I've even had breakfast. Something I rarely do. But I did it today, and with such pleasure! The oil was sizzling in the pan before I cracked two eggs—very carefully so as to not damage the yolk membrane—and as the whites hardened, those two balls shone a bright yellow. The butter spread on my bread was yellow with a shiny surface, and the apricot jam was also such a fragrant yellow, that the yellow color in the plates on the table seemed to have a taste of its own, one that it had never had before and would never have again. I put the white paper napkin in the plate, and my phone rang. I picked it up at the first ring, I was expecting this call. She's the one who's calling, but I will be the one to speak first.

"Hello, my beast," I say.

"Good morning."

Her voice is the yellowest in the world. I can't say more, you have to hear it to understand.

"When are we going to see each other?" I ask, although we had already agreed this during our last date.

"I've called to say that we can't see each other today."

I gasp. I won't survive. I've waited two days.

"I don't want to hear any of it," my throat seems dry. I must not let her know that my throat is dry.

"Your throat seems dry," she almost whispers, "Drink some water."

"I don't want to hear any of it," my voice grows stronger. Her scorn, once again, gives me strength.

"I have to take my mother to the doctor," she mumbles. That's exactly what she does – she mumbles; only she can whisper so softly and clearly.

"Take her," I say, "We'll see each other after that."

"It could take a while."

"So what? I'll wait."

"Don't you have any other problems besides me?"

"You know I don't."

"You do," she doesn't believe me, and it's a good thing she can't see my face as I blush.

"We must see each other," my whole mouth seems dry now, "Today."

"Well, we can't meet at noon, anyway."

"We can meet in the afternoon."

"In that case…" she's thinking out loud, "I'm going to take mother to the summerhouse after the clinic."

"We can take her together," I am gleeful, "You can finally introduce us."

"No," this is one of those cases when her "no" is a double "no".

"We'll get to know each other when you decide it's best," I say, feigning obedience.

"So, we're going to the doctor… then back home to get some things… then to the summerhouse…" I like it when she thinks out loud. But then she's quiet. Simply quiet. And I don't like it when she's quiet. "At around eight," she says finally.

"Eight?"

"I'll stay at your place tonight. Drink some water so that your throat doesn't dry up."

I'm already drinking water and trying to keep myself from imagining it – all night by my side, with me…

"At eight… where's the summerhouse? I can come and pick you up."

"No," it's one of those "no"-s again. "Mother shouldn't see you."

"But…"

"Don't interrupt," what was she doing, ordering me about? "You can wait for me at the 96-kilometer marker on the highway… near the oak tree that was struck by lightning. Take a cab there."

"Wouldn't it be better to take my car?"

"I'll have my car with me. Bye!"

I sit and look at my yellow breakfast. "Bye" – I repeat her last word and know that it, too, is yellow.

* * *

Before entering the office, I call Badger. She picks up at the first ring, she was expecting this call. I'm the one who's calling, but she speaks first.

"Good day," she says.

"Good day, my angel."

She laughs; her laugh irritates me more than usual today.

"When are we going to see each other?"

"I've called to say that..." I stretch out my words, let her chew her nails in tension.

"We're not going to see each other?" panicked at the pause I had inserted, she tried to finish my sentence, and I know that she is sighing now.

"At a different time."

"Is that all?" she must be smiling happily. I get more irritated.

"I can't see you in the evening. But at noon..."

"Noon," she seems to echo.

"Not where we had decided to meet," I wait to hear what she has to say. She is quiet. "Come to my place."

"Where?" She can't believe what she's hearing.

"I'll wait for you at home. Bye."

I don't know why but I'm convinced that she must have repeated the word "bye" after hanging up. But no matter how many times she repeats it, she won't know that the word is yellow in color.

I left the office forty minutes before noon. I told my boss that I'd finish up the designs at home and bring them in tomorrow. Of course I'll bring them in, I'd finished them two days ago, the project is ready. But there's no need for him to know that.

The doorbell sounds so frightened and timid that I give up on my initial intention—making her wait at the door—knowing well that she was chewing her nails with emotion. I open the door wide. It's Badger, and because she's holding a paper-wrapped package, her nails have been spared.

"Come in," I stand to one side and watch how she rubs against the wall as she walks in, and then hands me the package with a shy movement.

"What is it?" I can't look away from her eyes.

"Guess," she tries to smile.

"Oranges?" I see how her face brightens.

"How did you know?"

"I don't know," and I smirk to myself. After my yellow breakfast this morning, what else could it have been? Only oranges.

"This was how I imagined your place would be," she's walking around the room, looking at the shelves.

"Exactly like this?" my voice grows thorny, despite myself. "Have you seen many apartments that are only full of shelves, not counting the bed and a few chairs?"

"I've never seen one," she shrugs her shoulders in a confident sort of way, "Which is why I imagined it like this."

"Well, the logic of that argument is all screwed up, but… bingo!" I pick up the package and turn it over. The oranges roll onto the floor. Six oranges. I can't stand the number six.

"Don't touch them," I warn her, and she pulls back her hand. "Let' them stay on the floor. They're like…" I can't find the word.

"They're like you that way," she says, and I stare in surprise. This girl is becoming more enigmatic through the confidence that seems to be pulsing in her with each minute.

"Do you want some coffee?" I look at her hands. He small fingers, almost transparent at the nails, have balled up into fists. Catching the direction of my gaze, she manages to unclench them, but I'd already seen too much…

"I don't want any, but I'll have some."

Why did she say that?

"I can offer tea if you don't want coffee," I say and justify this to myself – everyone has the right to a choice, even she. If she chooses tea, then I won't need the powder in the syringe. At least, not today…

"No, coffee's fine. I want to see what the coffee you make tastes like," she seems to be mocking me.

"Well, if that's what you want… you said it yourself."

"I said for you to make it," she says and walks to the balcony door.

"Where are you going?" I manage to grab her hand.

"Let's have coffee on the balcony," she smiles.

That was all I needed at this point. Nobody was supposed to see us together… On my balcony at that… Having coffee…

"We'll have coffee…" I take her to the bedroom door. "Go in, we'll have coffee in bed."

She goes in without looking at me and closes the door. I go to the kitchen and do not spare the coffee – the coffee I make and that she will drink needs to be very bitter. All that remains is filling the powder from the syringe in one of the cups…

Two hours later, Badger turns around and hugs me before leaving. She kisses me and leaves without saying a word. I bring her cup from the bedroom to the kitchen and wash it. Then I wash it again. Then I break it, reduce it to small pieces and pour it into the toilet bowl. After flushing several times, there's nothing left. Nothing.

Two months ago, an old woman walked up to me on the street and said that I could pay the parrot that was perched on her shoulder and it would take out a rolled-up piece of paper from the basket and tell my fortune. I was alone back then, down on my luck, seeing a therapist and contemplating suicide. I would have damned the old woman to hell if that had not been the case. The parrot took out a rolled-up piece of paper.

"Don't open it yet," the old woman warned me, "You have to do what it says. If you're not going to do it, you can take your money back and return the paper."

I pushed back her hand.

"Promise me," she was agitated.

"I promise, now get lost… What's going on?"

"You've promised," she said, turned around and left quickly. Or fled.

Within two months starting today, you have to seek and kill someone, in order to hold on to the happiness you'll find.

I crumpled up the paper and put it in my pocket. There were more and more crazies in the city.

I had just gotten into the office when my boss called. I went. I'd written up a letter of resignation just in case. It was in my pocket.

"Come in, sit down… How are you?" When was the last time I'd seen him smiling, and to me at that? I could not recall.

"Thanks… fine," and since the letter was in my pocket, my voice sounded—or so I thought—sarcastic.

"Fine? How can you be fine? You've been stuck in the same position for so many years, no career progress, no opportunities…" Was he thinking out loud? And then he examined me, his face no longer smiling. "I'm giving you the project to design the administrative building."

I couldn't believe it. I couldn't comprehend it.

"The deadlines are tight. Will you manage?"

I knew that the only word I could say at that moment was the one he wanted to hear.

"I'll manage."

He smiled with satisfaction and led me to the door.

"This could end up being a great success for you, and you must do everything to hold on to that success," he shook my hand.

I tried to recall where I had heard a thought that sounded similar to those words…

A week later, I found my Beast on a street. She walked past me, took a few steps and… twisted her ankle, I barely managed to hold her up. I held her. For a moment. Then I took her to the nearest café and the waiter put ice on her ankle. Then we had coffee, then wine… She told me her name, but I wasn't concentrating, I had already decided to call her angel. When I told her, she laughed. A loud, confusing laugh.

"I'm nothing like an angel. Perhaps I'd agree to be called Monster, or at least… a Little Beast."

I did not like the fact that she already knew what women eventually turn into for the men who desire them.

I did not realize how life had started to surge within me again. The project began to take shape, I already knew that I would be finished with it two days before the deadline. And my Little Beast… There had been many women in my life before her, but there could be nobody after her. I understood this the first time I had possessed her. And it was only the following morning that I remembered… I had to hold on to this happiness. It was foolishness… But I began to look for the old woman and her parrot on the streets. I knew that I would not be able to find them, and with each day, I began to leave the house with more resolve. One month remained when I saw the girl I needed in a café. Nothing special about how she looked, her face covered in freckles… colorless, like a badger. I walked up to her. When I asked if I could sit on the chair next to hers, she looked at me in surprise. I realized that I had been the first person in her life to ask such a thing. Had I decided to approach her a month ago it would not have worked – I was too stressed, too melancholic and full of failure to interest her, much less charm her. But that had been a month ago. But now I had a promising project and a Little Beast… I asked for her phone number and, seeing her reaction, I realize that she thinks I'll forget her face and her number as soon as I leave the café. That was why, when she left her house the following morning and saw me standing there with a single rose, she froze in place, the poor thing. I spent the first five minutes calmly explaining how easy it was to get an address once you know a person's phone number. She alternated between smiling and blushing, but I had the calendar in mind… twenty-nine days to go. She took the rose and told me her name. I didn't hear it, I told her that I would call her Angel. She smiled, as if this were perfectly normal, and did not flinch. I guess she took what I was saying seriously. I opened the car door and, seeing how awkwardly she sat, named her Badger. She could not hope for anything better.

The taxi driver was an old man, but not someone who was fed up with life. He talked the whole way, joking and telling me stories about his grandchildren… He got a double tip and returned to the city. It was seven forty. I had intentionally arrived early. I'm walking along the forest path I know well, the one that starts right at the edge of the highway and, fifty meters later, I'm at the oak tree that had been struck by lightning. My Little Beast and I had enjoyed each other there once. We had escaped from the city, from everyone there, and we had spent the whole day together… For the first time out in nature, under the blazing light of the sun… I had not understood why she'd asked me to park the car on the edge of the road. She had stepped out and walked to the forest. I had followed. We walked in silence. We got to the oak tree. She turned around, embraced me and pushed me to the ground. Beneath my back, the dry leaves from several years crunched with satisfaction. She unbuckled my belt and sat down on me… It was only when everything was over that I realized how I had submitted to her…

I sit down on what was once an oak but is now a partly burned piece of wood. I try not to think about how Badger is probably suffocating right now and unable to understand what is going on. An absurd thought occurs to me – what if Badger realizes at the last moment why the coffee was so bitter? If she does, then she'll realize why I named her Angel, and why she did not resist this name. Perhaps the frightening discovery that angels are meant to be sacrificed was now but a memory in her frozen eyes…

That powder had an advantage – its effect kicks in after several hours. And nobody ever saw me with Badger. Except for at the café and the following day. And that was such a long time ago… I'd rather think of the night ahead of me. My Little Beast and I are meeting in secret, I've asked to meet her mother so many times. It's not the right time yet, she says with that yellow smile. I look at my watch, she'll be here any minute. I'll be able to hear the purring of the car engine first, then the sound of a door opening and closing, and then she'll appear. I suddenly realize what it means to be dying of desire. And I decide to tell her about Badger one day. Perhaps that will be twenty or thirty years from now, when our children will have children of their own, when we'll be living peacefully together, old but not yet having had our fill of each other. And I'll tell her about Badger and how, thanks to her, I managed to hold on to this happiness. She'll understand. She must understand.

It grows unexpectedly dark. I look up and see that the clouds have clumped together and blackened the sky. It's going to rain… And that is when I see the gun barrel aimed at me. And then a dull sound, and I manage to see the partly-burned oak stump coming up at me…

The gun was thrown in a reservoir. The car, a rental, was returned. She walked a few streets and got into her own car, and went home. On the way, she was trying not to remember how clever she had been in twisting her ankle and landing in that loser's arms. He had taken her to the nearest café… ice… coffee… wine… and everything had ended up exactly as planned. Of course, she had been searching for two weeks before she saw him and realized that she had found the person she needed. Nothing special about how he looked, his face covered in freckles… colorless. She realized how she had clenched up inside when that loser had called her Angel – he did not yet know that angels are meant to be sacrificed. Later, she had been surprised that he had shown no resistance to her words – "Perhaps I'd agree to be called Monster, or at least… a Little Beast." Perhaps he knew already that he was signing a death wish. When she looked at his cold eyes staring up to the sky, an absurd thought occurred to her – what if he realized that she had been calling him Colorless Angel all this time?

* * *

She walked into her house and took out the paper the crazy old woman's parrot had given her. She burned it in an ashtray, reading the burning words for the last time, "…hold on to the happiness…" She had done everything right. She poured the ash into the toilet bowl. After flushing several times, there was nothing left. Nothing.

It was the phone. She picked it up on the first ring and was once again not surprised at how she had been waiting for his voice. And although he had called, she would be the first to speak.

"Hello, darling."

"Hello," the voice at the other end of the phone did not have the same tone as it did everyday… or so it seemed.

"When are we going to see each other?" asked the woman who had fired three bullets into the skull of a colorless loser a few hours ago. She asked and held her breath – what if the person at the other end of the phone postponed their date? And as she waited to hear his response, she felt her soul going cold.

Goodbye, Bird

by Aram Pachyan

For a twenty-eight-year-old young man who returned from the army several years ago but has yet to reacclimatize to ordinary life, every step, gesture, word, and vision is a revelation, which takes him back to the beginning, to a time when reality had lost its shape, and turned into a new and imperceptible world. In his imagination, he embodies a number of different characters, he feels the presence of his girlfriend again, and remembers friends from his childhood and from the army, who are now gone. This is a book of questions, and the answers to these questions are to be found by the reader. The novel is like a puzzle which needs to be pieced together, and the picture is not complete until the last piece is in place, until the last word of the book has been read.

This book was published with the support of the Ministry of Culture of the Republic of Armenia under the "Armenian Literature in Translation" Program.

Buy it > www.glagoslav.com

Little Zinnobers
by Elena Chizhova

Is it possible to cultivate fundamental human values if you live in a totalitarian state? A teacher who instigates the school theatre sets out to prove that it is. But while the pupils rehearse Shakespeare's tragedies and comedies under her ever-vigilant eye, Soviet life makes its brutal adjustments. This can be called a book about love, the tough kind of love that gets you through life, and death.

Zinnobers is especially fascinating for British readers as we see Shakespeare's famous sonnets and plays are touchingly brought to life by the Russian children and their gifted teacher, the novel's heroine. The teacher applies some of the playwright's satire to the socio-political situation of the USSR, using her English lessons to teach her students life's broader lessons, too.

Echoes of the Soviet Union can be felt in our own society today: the people find themselves increasingly at odds with the politicians' hypocrisy, 'big brother' is watching us through thousands of CCTVs, and political correctness determines what we can and cannot say...

Buy it > www.glagoslav.com

A Brown Man in Russia
Lessons Learned on the Trans-Siberian
by Vijay Menon

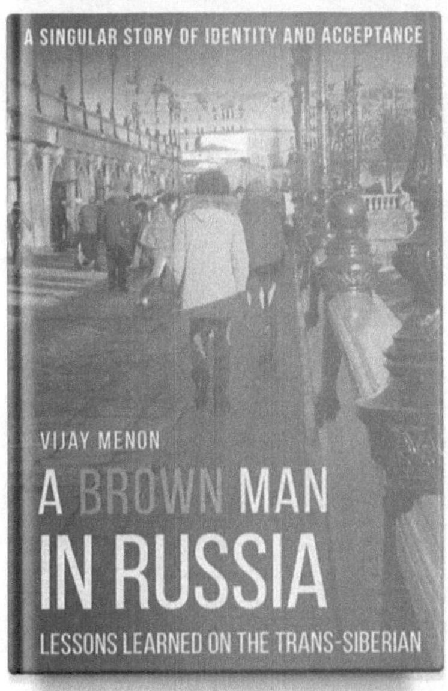

A Brown Man in Russia describes the fantastical travels of a young, colored American traveler as he backpacks across Russia in the middle of winter via the Trans-Siberian. The book is a hybrid between the curmudgeonly travelogues of Paul Theroux and the philosophical works of Robert Pirsig. Styled in the vein of Hofstadter, the author lays out a series of absurd, but true stories followed by a deeper rumination on what they mean and why they matter. Each chapter presents a vivid anecdote from the perspective of the fumbling traveler and concludes with a deeper lesson to be gleaned. For those who recognize the discordant nature of our world in a time ripe for demagoguery and for those who want to make it better, the book is an all too welcome antidote. It explores the current global climate of despair over differences and outputs a very different message – one of hope and shared understanding. At times surreal, at times inappropriate, at times hilarious, and at times deeply human, A Brown Man in Russia is a reminder to those who feel marginalized, hopeless, or endlessly divided that harmony is achievable even in the most unlikely of places.

Girls, be Good

by Bojan Babić

"Girls, be good" is an omnibus novel that consists of twenty short stories connected by a single framing narrative: just after the fall of the Berlin wall, foreign investors feel good about the investment climate in Eastern Europe and decide to open a huge toy factory in ex-Yugoslavia, where they are going to produce a hit range of toys designed for girls: small, plush lemurs called Aya, that will be sold all over the world. Before long, though, their optimism starts to feel out of place - the war in Yugoslavia begins, and the factory, having only produced one edition of the toys, has to shut down production...

Death of the Snake Catcher

by Ak Welsapar

This book features people from one of the most closed countries of today's world, where the passage of time resembles the passage of a caravan through the waterless desert. This world has been recreated by a true-born son of that mysterious country, a Turkmen who, at the will of fate, has now been living for a quarter of a century in snowy Scandinavia. Is that not why two different worlds come together in *Ryazan horseradish and Tula gingerbread*, to come apart in *Love in Lilac*, in which a student from the non-free world falls in love with a girl from the West?

In the story *Death of the Snake Catcher*, an old snake catcher meets one on one with a giant cobra in the heart of the desert. In the dialogue between them the author unveils the age-old interdependence of Man and untamed nature, where the fear and mistrust of the strong and the hopes and apprehensions of the weak change places but co-exist as ever. *Egyptian night of fear*, in which a boy goes to an Eastern bazaar and falls into the clutches of depraved forces, is created in the writer's characteristic style of magical realism, while the novella Altynai celebrates first love, radiant and sad, pure as virgin snow.

Buy it > www.glagoslav.com

Leo Tolstoy – Flight from Paradise

by Pavel Basinsky

Over a hundred years ago, something truly outrageous occurred at Yasnaya Polyana. Count Leo Tolstoy, a famous author aged eighty-two at the time, took off, destination unknown. Since then, the circumstances surrounding the writer's whereabouts during his final days and his eventual death have given rise to many myths and legends. In this book, popular Russian writer and reporter Pavel Basinsky delves into the archives and presents his interpretation of the situation prior to Leo Tolstoy's mysterious disappearance. Basinsky follows Leo Tolstoy throughout his life, right up to his final moments. Reconstructing the story from historical documents, he creates a visionary account of the events that led to the Tolstoys' family drama.

Flight from Paradise will be of particular interest to international researchers studying Leo Tolstoy's life and works, and is highly recommended to a broader audience worldwide.

Buy it > www.glagoslav.com

- *Don't Call me a Victim!* by Dina Yafasova
- *Poetin (Dutch Edition)* by Chris Hutchins
  and Alexander Korobko
- *A History of Belarus* by Lubov Bazan
- *Children's Fashion of the Russian Empire* by Alexander Vasiliev
- *Empire of Corruption - The Russian National Pastime* by Vladimir
  Soloviev
- *Heroes of the 90s - People and Money. The Modern History
  of Russian Capitalism*
- *Fifty Highlights from the Russian Literature (Dutch Edition)* by
  Maarten Tengbergen
- *Bajesvolk (Dutch Edition)* by Mikhail Khodorkovsky
- *Tsarina Alexandra's Diary (Dutch Edition)*
- *Myths about Russia* by Vladimir Medinskiy
- *Boris Yeltsin - The Decade that Shook the World* by Boris Minaev
- *A Man Of Change - A study of the political life
  of Boris Yeltsin*
- *Sberbank - The Rebirth of Russia's Financial Giant*
  by Evgeny Karasyuk
- *To Get Ukraine* by Oleksandr Shyshko
- *Asystole* by Oleg Pavlov
- *Gnedich* by Maria Rybakova
- *Marina Tsvetaeva - The Essential Poetry*
- *Multiple Personalities* by Tatyana Shcherbina
- *The Investigator* by Margarita Khemlin
- *The Exile* by Zinaida Tulub
- *Leo Tolstoy – Flight from paradise* by Pavel Basinsky
- *Moscow in the 1930* by Natalia Gromova
- *Laurus (Dutch edition)* by Evgenij Vodolazkin
- *Prisoner* by Anna Nemzer
- *The Crime of Chernobyl - The Nuclear Goulag*
  by Wladimir Tchertkoff
- *Alpine Ballad* by Vasil Bykau
- *The Complete Correspondence of Hryhory Skovoroda*
- *The Tale of Aypi* by Ak Welsapar
- *Selected Poems* by Lydia Grigorieva
- *The Fantastic Worlds of Yuri Vynnychuk*

- *The Garden of Divine Songs and Collected Poetry of Hryhory Skovoroda*
- *Adventures in the Slavic Kitchen: A Book of Essays with Recipes*
- *Seven Signs of the Lion* by Michael M. Naydan
- *Forefathers' Eve* by Adam Mickiewicz
- *One-Two* by Igor Eliseev
- *Girls, be Good* by Bojan Babić
- *Time of the Octopus* by Anatoly Kucherena
- *The Grand Harmony* by Bohdan Ihor Antonych
- *The Selected Lyric Poetry Of Maksym Rylsky*
- *The Shining Light* by Galymkair Mutanov
- *The Frontier: 28 Contemporary Ukrainian Poets - An Anthology*
- *Acropolis - The Wawel Plays* by Stanisław Wyspiański
- *Contours of the City* by Attyla Mohylny
- *Conversations Before Silence: The Selected Poetry of Oles Ilchenko*
- *The Secret History of my Sojourn in Russia* by Jaroslav Hašek
- *Mirror Sand - An Anthology of Russian Short Poems in English Translation* (A Bilingual Edition)
- *Maybe We're Leaving* by Jan Balaban
- *Death of the Snake Catcher* by Ak WelsaparRichard Govett
- *A Brown Man in Russia - Perambulations Through A Siberian Winter* by Vijay Menon
- *Hard Times* by Ostap Vyshnia
- *The Flying Dutchman* by Anatoly Kudryavitsky
- *Nikolai Gumilev's Africa* by Nikolai Gumilev
- *Combustions* by Srđan Srdić
- *The Sonnets* by Adam Mickiewicz
- *Dramatic Works* by Zygmunt Krasiński
- *Four Plays* by Juliusz Słowacki
- *Little Zinnobers* by Elena Chizhova
- *A Flame Out at Sea* by Dmitry Novikov
- *We Are Building Capitalism! Moscow in Transition 1992-1997*
- *The Hemingway Game* by Evgeny Grishkovets
- *The Nuremberg Trials* by Alexander Zvyagintsev
- *Jesus' Cat* by Grig
- *I Want a Baby and Other Plays* by Sergei Tretyakov
- *Biography of Sergei Prokofiev* by Igor Vishnevetsky
- *Mikhail Bulgakov: The Life and Times* by Marietta Chudakova
- *Duel* by Borys Antonenko-Davydovych

More coming soon...